Riding the Tide

The Inner Circle - Book 1

Rogue London & N.M. McGregor

ROTTIE BOOKS LLC

Published by Rottie Books LLC
A Tennessee Organization

Copyright ©2025 Rogue London and N.M. McGregor.
All rights are reserved.

No part of this publication may be reproduced, stored in a retrieval system and/or made public in any form or by any means, electronic, mechanical, photocopying, recording or otherwise, without the prior written permission of the publisher. deborah@rottiebooks.com.

This book is fiction. Names, places, locations and events are either created in the author's imagination or are used fictitiously. Any resemblance to actual persons, places and events is purely coincidental.

Blurb by Alluring Blurbs
Cover art by – Rogue London and Western Sky

First printing edition December 31, 2017
West End Montana by N.M. McGregor
Published by Nadine Jolly - CanEngrave Signs and Printing, Surrey, B.C. Canada
ISBN: 978-0-9958974-2-7

Second printing edition April, 29, 2018
West End Montana by N.M. McGregor
ASIN B06Y5QY3QK

Third printing edition January 28, 2018
West End Montana by N.M. McGregor
ASIN B07K7XT5P3

ISBN: 979-8-9912911-9-4 (ebook)
ISBN: 979-8-9925234-0-9 (paperback)

Contents

Author Warning	VII
Chapter 1	1
Chapter 2	7
Chapter 3	13
Chapter 4	21
Chapter 5	33
Chapter 6	37
Chapter 7	47
Chapter 8	49
Chapter 9	61
Chapter 10	67
Chapter 11	77
Chapter 12	93
Chapter 13	101
Chapter 14	109

Chapter 15	123
Chapter 16	135
Chapter 17	149
Chapter 18	165
Chapter 19	177
Chapter 20	191
Chapter 21	203
Chapter 22	211
Chapter 23	225
Chapter 24	231
Chapter 25	243
Chapter 26	249
Chapter 27	257
Acknowledgements	267
About Rogue London	269
About N.M. McGregor	271
About the Publisher	273

It might be all in the journey, but some destinations you can never come back from.

I know exactly how I got here. Growing up, and navigating life isn't easy, especially when you have a reputation to protect. Learning who to trust, and making new enemies, often felt like walking through a minefield.

Sure, I had my brothers who were sometimes more like parents than siblings. So annoying. But that didn't make anything easy. Especially not for a sassy, mouthy, take-no-shit-chick like me.

A string of events no one my age should have to deal with is how I got here. Standing on the edge, with a choice that, once made, can never be undone. My crown has toppled from my head too many times to count and, this time, I don't know if there's any coming back.

This book was previously published as West End Montana under the pen name of N.M. McGregor and has been re-titled, given a new cover, been re-edited, and parts of the book have been changed from the original story.

Warning:

This is my story. It's gritty, raw, and authentically me. I'm an 80's chick. I know, we're all so old now! But back in the day, the world was a much different place.

In the 80's we didn't have supervision, we were feral, wild creatures roaming the streets and getting into shit we probably shouldn't have been. We grew up well before our time and experienced things at much younger ages than now.

The laws and restrictions you have always known didn't exist for us. No one cared about drinking or drugs or even where we were as long as it wasn't in jail or a hospital.

You're going to read this story and probably think it's some sort of fantasy land, because you can't imagine a world without your parents hovering and a thousand and one rules for you to follow. But it's an authentic depiction of the world I grew up in. No, it isn't for the faint of heart, but go ahead and dive in…. Or are you chicken?

"A gripping tale of self discovery and perseverance. Montana's journey had me enthralled from the very start. It still lives rent free in my head" – International Bestselling Author, L.G. Knight

Chapter 1

November 1981

I plunged into the icy sea. Enough was enough! No more pain, no more loss. Right now, at this moment, this was my world, and my choice as to how my story ended. I waded out into the ocean, doing my best to ignore the fact that the water was freezing.

It was November first, and in our Canadian climate... of course, it was freezing, but hey, who wanted to drown themselves in warm tropical water, anyway? No, it was much better this way, I convinced myself as I waded further.

From somewhere, I heard a voice call me. "Montana." I was up to my chin in the water and turned to see where the voice was coming from and who it belonged to. Way up on the beach, I saw a red Mustang. I recognized it, of course. It belonged to my brother Dan.

Of course he and my other two brothers had been looking for me. I had left home a few days before with a plan to spend time with one of my west side buddies. A plan I hadn't shared with anyone from home. I had attended a Halloween party with them last night and afterward hadn't gone home or back to my friend Shelley's, which I had arranged to do.

Instead, I had slept in the woods and was now scrambling to get into the icy depths before anyone could find me. Call me a coward, but I wanted to choose when and how, and my reasons were my own. I felt my right as a human trumped their right as my family to stop me.

I dove beneath the icy waves, reaching for the bottom while holding a rock I had carried out with me from shore. As I sank deeper my life flashed in picture cards, one after the other, with the last year and a half playing a predominant role in the images that danced behind my closed eyes, starting with Adam, and the car.

April 1980

What an awesome movie! John Travolta as Danny Zucko was so hot and Olivia Newton-John, I mean at the end like "wow", she was amazing. The two of them were as opposite as could be, but when they met in the summer, there was no one else around to point that out, all they saw was their mutual attraction. Their different backgrounds didn't matter until school started, then it all changed.

Everyone had been raving about *Grease,* so I had to see it, and I loved it! The coolest part was the school; it was so big, and they had activities that a little high school like mine would never have. I was deep in thought comparing these differences as I walked home from the theatre, and so caught up that I didn't immediately notice I was being followed.

Someone in a black car was trailing me, in a black 280Z to be specific, and I didn't recognize it as belonging to anyone I knew. Just as I was about to take a turnoff and slip away to a darker path home, the car suddenly turned the corner and went out of sight. As the possible threat seemed to be gone, I went back to my musings.

Sandy (Olivia Newton-John) had blue eyes like me, but that's where the resemblance ended. I had a long, lean, athletic body with shoulder-length auburn hair, a sprinkling of freckles, and an impish grin that had trouble written all over it, while Sandy was the ultra-slim, dainty blond with the wholesome smile I wished I had.

Sandy seemed to live in a world where nice suburban neighborhoods existed, and every family had two cars, two kids, and a cabin on the lake. My family, which consisted of me, my three brothers, and my dad, lived in the city. Right in the heart of downtown Vancouver, the West End: Land of apartments, and literally stuffed full of the largest selection of people.

Not that I didn't like how or where I lived. I mean, we lived where all the action was. It was the best place to people-watch, surrounded by the beauty of Stanley Park and English Bay just a few blocks away. These natural resources helped to take our minds off our dysfunctional lifestyle. I say dysfunctional because our dad was only home six weeks out of the year. Still having a dad made us a minority where we lived.

Our world was one of single parents, pimps, flashers, and even sniper fire from time to time. My mind was spinning with the comparisons between my life and Sandy's, many of which had nothing to do with the actual movie, but more of a comparison of the bigger picture, of us versus them.

Smiling at this realization, my thoughts spiraled once again as I congratulated myself on this small epiphany, failing to remember about the car that had been following me—or at least I had forgotten temporarily—but there it was again, just up ahead at the corner, idling like it was waiting for someone. Friend or foe, it was too late to run regardless, as it stood between me and home. Damn! Ace was going to kill me for letting my guard down, if this person didn't kill me first.

Ace was my eldest brother and guardian since our dad worked so far away. He was six feet four with an athletic, football player build. Most people were very intimidated by Ace; he could look really scary when he wanted to. But he wasn't scary at all unless you'd really screwed up and were a recipient of *the look*. Ace had cultivated this *look*, and if you were on the receiving end of it, you knew you were in deep trouble.

But like I said, he wasn't scary for the most part, just cranky and overburdened with responsibilities that no one his age should have. The hair on my arms stood as I approached the car, my breath hitching with adrenalin going into overdrive. I noticed the window was down on the passenger side. Maybe whoever it was just needed directions.

"Hey, aren't you Danny's little sister?"

Relief flooded through me, but it was short lived. Sure, whoever this dude was, at least he knew my family, but what if he was an enemy?

"Who wants to know?" I asked, my deadpan voice filled with enough edge to let him know I wouldn't be easy prey.

"Ease up," he answered. "My name is Adam, and I go to art school with your brother Danny. I was at the movies and thought you might need a ride home. After all, it's late and most likely no one knows where you are... am I right?"

I didn't answer right away, because he called me on something that I only allowed friends to know about me, unless Danny had been talking about his bratty sister with this guy, which made me ponder exactly who he was? On the flip side of my cautious thoughts was an entirely different process-gorgeous guy, nice car... no tough choice there. "Cool," I finally answered as I hopped into the passenger side.

I remained mute while he chatted happily about the movie we had both just seen. Being hyper vigilant allowed me to take in his characteristics which said a lot about him. The car was clean, like new clean yet the model was a year old. Between us was an open notebook and from my angle I could read what appeared to be a poem. Being the nosy person I am, I read it.

As the driver spoke aloud, I heard his voice speaking the words as I read them. His smoky tone had the tiniest of accents that imbued the words of the page with a clear strong message. His written piece of magic entitled, "You," was really good and very expressive. I glanced over to study his features while he continued to speak and was blown away by just how handsome he was. Super gorgeous, and I guessed he was about six feet tall. His thigh muscles bunched as he drove, along with his right forearm as he shifted the gear stick. My eyes trailed up to his face and admired his green eyes and a bone structure that reminded me of a Michelangelo statue.

In looks he rivaled my brother Danny, who until this moment I had thought was the most gorgeous guy alive. "Adam", he'd said his name was. Like the first man God had created in his image, or so the story went. "Hey, Adam, are you into literary art, or just the visual stuff like Danny?"

"I love all art, Montana, but out of the literary arena, I'd have to say that poetry is my favourite. I write poetry all the time. How about you?"

His words warmed me up inside. He wasn't only perfect on the outside, but I was quickly beginning to see that the inside matched. "Oh yes," I answered, a smile tugging at my lips. "I write all the time. I find it's a good release, especially for pent up frustrations."

He drew his eyes from the road to me for a brief moment and I felt myself blush. Was he drawing a conclusion regarding my statement of *pent up frustrations?* Until that moment we were just two people sharing a ride. What I'd said opened up a further discussion, one I was wholly uncomfortable having, especially with Mr. Sexy in the seat beside me.

Chapter 2

November 1, 1981

I was freezing and my head felt like it would explode. I knew I was close... just a few more seconds, and I would be gone, and finally be with my mother.

"Montana!"

Someone was shaking me, and I could feel something on my lips. No, my mind screamed, don't bring me back, I refuse! This is the end I choose... but I was too weak to fight off my rescuer.

"No," I managed to croak out in a barely audible whisper. "No," I repeated, my mind shifting from the present to the movie playing in my head as I let go. I settled into the pictures again, enjoying these memories. It was like hanging out with an old friend, a welcome friend.

April 1980

I wondered what Ace would say after seeing Adam drop me off at home. Most likely, he would be pissed off with me. He always was, and said I was much too spontaneous for my own good. If Adam dropped me off at the end of my street Ace wouldn't know I took a ride home with a complete stranger. When we arrived at my block I gestured to him to pull over. I got out and leaned back in the car to thank him. Adam beat me to it, offering me a brilliant smile. "It's been real," he said. Chuckling, I assumed, at my miffed expression.

"Yeah. Thanks." I closed the door and then sort of floated down the street toward home, the effect of having spent time with a guy who genuinely piqued my interest. To any passersby I looked perfectly normal, but on the inside I was floating, swishing my arms and leaping after being with him. He was refreshing in a way that kinda woke me up inside.

When I arrived home, I beelined for my bedroom, flopped down on my bed, and replayed the entire ride home with Adam. My reverie didn't last long however as moments later my door flew open.

"Montana Margaret Stanford, where have you been, and who have you been with?"

"Oh, hi, big brother. How are you doing? I'm sorry I didn't hear you when I came in. I was focusing on a homework assignment I have due Monday."

"Mo, when have you ever worried about a homework assignment, especially days before it's due?" he asked, as his eyes narrowed into a glinting stare. "I repeat, where were you and who were you with?"

"Um, I went to the movies."

"Alone?" he asked.

"Yes," I squeaked in response, looking anywhere but at him. "There were other kids I knew walking home, so it's all good."

"Who?" he asked, taking a step closer.

I cringed, who, who, damn if I knew, think, Montana, who could you have walked home with that he couldn't check with the next day?

"Hey Ace, what's up?"

We both turned to see our friend Eddy standing in my doorway.

"Montana was just about to explain to me who she walked home from the movies with," Ace answered, turning his focus back to me.

"Oh. Well, did you tell him you were with me?" Eddy gave me a meaningful look. Ace and I both stared at Eddy and a grin slowly spread across my face. Ace looked unconvinced but didn't say anything as Eddy continued.

"I saw Mo there, and after my show was over, my friends and I met up with her. I left her at the corner while I said goodbye to my buddies... hope that's okay."

Ace's gaze bore into Eddy's eyes. Eddy didn't blink, didn't flinch. He would make a great cop one day, I mused. Thankfully, he was usually on team Montana. After what seemed like an eternity had passed, Ace seemed to buy the story.

"Thanks, Eddy, for doing that. You know how reckless she can be." With that, he walked out and closed my door. Eddy and I waited for a moment, listening to his retreating steps, and we both let out a sigh of relief.

"Eddy, have I ever told you that you're my best friend in the whole world? Thanks so much."

"No probs." he said, with a chuckle. "I think I'm the only one who can fool him... so who was the good-looking guy in the hot car, anyway?"

My face went beet red. Good Lord, he had seen me! What could I tell him about Adam? There really wasn't anything to tell... except... well... I wanted and hoped I would see him again and that wish I decided to keep to myself. "A friend of Danny's from art school," I said, and left it at that.

Eddy didn't push for more which is one of the many reasons why he is my closest guy friend. Not just me, he was friends with all my brothers. Age-wise, he was older than me and my twin, Alex, but younger than my next oldest brother, Danny. I don't remember who befriended whom first, but he'd been around our family since before I was born. His family lived three houses down from us, and he was an only child. My mom had loved Eddy like he was one of her own, so we all accepted him as a brother.

When our mother got sick, Eddy's mom had been really kind to us and had kept us fed while our dad was busy taking care of mom. A while after mom had passed, dad needed to make more money to pay off the bills that had stacked up during that time.

He went off to work in the east, a job he'd done before meeting mom, and Eddy's mom made sure the four of us ate and had what we needed. As we'd grown and became more and more independent, time spent at Eddy's had become less and less. But if I was ever hungry, I knew exactly where to go.

Chapter 3

November 1981

Mom... that had brought up a well of emotions. The pictures momentarily ceased while I reflected on Mom. She'd died when Alex and I were little, seven-ish, I guess, but I didn't like thinking about it. In no reality did I want to relive the pain; there had been enough of that to last a lifetime.

Thinking about mom was like taking a deep dive into an endless pool of uncertainty. Ace didn't cry at the funeral and neither did I. Our dad, Danny and Alex had all cried like babies, but my oldest brother had resembled an ice sculpture. I remember touching him at one point to make sure he was still there. His blank gaze had landed on me and made me shudder at the time. I now realized he'd been unable to process the loss.

Now, so much has happened since she left us and in some ways, I often felt like an old lady. In my waking world, the first morning glance in the mirror was always a shock when I saw myself looking my age. I'd sigh with relief. Then a deeper look in my eyes showed the much older person I felt like, one who knew more than they should and experienced too much.

My brother, Alex, did as well and probably a lot of his came from being my twin as I was always the one that seemed to crash and fall while he sailed smoothly through most things. There were advantages and disadvantages, as I would find out later. We shared a connection I suspected would grow with time, just like it had expanded when we started playing music together.

Alex was near to me, I could feel him tugging at the edges of my consciousness. He was hurting and his pain was bringing me dangerously close to waking up.

My mind flowed back and forth like ocean currents as my memories jumped from past to present and back again.

I strove to put myself back under. Wherever I was – heaven, hell, or Earth – I wasn't ready to find out, so I pushed myself back to the pictures, and it picked up right where I had left off, just like releasing the pause button on the video machine.

April 1980

I decided to change the topic with Eddy and asked him if he remembered that time he had rescued me and my girlfriends at the local ice rink in the West End Community Centre. We laughed as I retold the story about Jim the bully.

My girlfriends and I had decided to go to Friday night skate. It would be my first time since having a full-length leg cast removed a few days previous. Ace probably wouldn't have approved but my doctor had said to start strengthening the muscles, which I interpreted as going skating. The rink was full that night, and we knew at least half the people there.

One big guy named Jim Tylor was there. He was a good skater and knew it. He skated around showing off and being a total jerk. Every time he came to a stop, he'd be close enough to spray people, covering their jeans with ice. More than one person was annoyed with his childish antics, and I wasn't the only one who wanted to see him humbled. He was intimidating, and bigger than most, so most of those sharing the ice with him did their best to ignore him.

Being me, I couldn't hold my temper back, especially when he stopped so sharply that the ice flicked up into a kid's face and he fell down. It was kinda the last straw for me as bullying was something I would never tolerate.

"You know you're a total jerk, right?"

He seemed amused by my outburst and continued on like he hadn't heard a word I said, but he was just biding his time. A few minutes later he managed to sneak up behind me and push me down on the ice. He knew, cause everyone knew, I'd just gotten that cast off and what could potentially happen if I got my knee injured again. Normally only my pride would have been hurt being caught off guard, and I would have gotten over that eventually. However, the pain that shot through my leg pushed me over the edge of "reasonable".

In true Montana fashion, I saw red and waited for the right moment to take my revenge. Thankfully, it didn't take long, as Jim was caught up in his reflection in the glass surrounding the rink. So infatuated with himself, that he completely missed me coming up behind him. As we came around the oval edge, I shoved as hard as I could and almost shouted with happiness as Jim went spiraling on his stomach down the ice and landed with a gentle bump against the side board. It was an epic moment and one that inspired a lot of laughter.

When he got back on his blades he came after me like a mad bull. The joke was over and the reality that I was about to get pulverized set in. I flew off the ice and headed for the girl's washroom and hid in the last stall, praying that the ice officials, who were my friends, wouldn't let Jim come in.

Minutes ticked by, and finally one of my girlfriends came in to tell me that Jim and a few guys had left, and the rink was closing. I wanted to stay and sleep on the bench. I just knew somewhere between here and home they would be waiting for me, but I was forced out of my safe haven a few minutes later.

My girlfriends lived in the opposite direction and headed for home, leaving me to determine my best route home. Because it was 10:30 at night, and winter, it would have been smart to take the regular route along the well lit main streets, and avoid any alleys where unsavory characters liked to lay in wait for the unsuspecting.

Being spotted by Jim was the last thing I wanted. I figured it would be easier to run from a druggie than a super angry athlete and chose the dark alley path instead. Yes it was potentially dangerous, but if I stuck tight to the buildings, I'd just be another shadow in the night.

Decision made: I snuck around the corner of the concrete building that housed the ice arena and the local library and stuck to the shadows. As I turned the corner there was Jim with three friends. I could have turned and run if I was a coward, but a true "West Ender" has the heart of a lion and we all knew that running only prolonged the inevitable. I crossed my arms and put on a brave face.

"Hey you," Jim shouted. His voice rang out in the silent darkness and I wondered if by chance someone might hear what was going down and investigate. The four of them made a ring around me and closed in. I was horrified to see one of my old boyfriends among them. I gave him a withering look and he dropped his eyes, his face going a bit red, clearly embarrassed to be part of the group waylaying me like I was some kind of criminal when really it was all Jim's fault in the first place.

"What do you want?" I asked in the toughest voice I could conjure up.

"Revenge," Jim said with an evil grin.

Shit! Think, Montana. How could I get out of being beat up? At least I hoped that was all they had planned for me. The look of glee in Jim's eyes made me nervous. I noticed the bully had his prize skates over his shoulder with no guards on the blades. An idea formulated in my mind to draw everyone's attention away from me. I grabbed the bully's skates so fast he didn't know what was happening.

"Let me go, or the skates are going on a trip across the concrete."

Jim snickered as if I didn't have the guts to do what I'd said. His smirk was like a dare I fully planned on living up to. I whirled the skates around in the air by their laces and chucked them as far and as I could. The high pitched grating of blades on concrete pierced the air. It was almost as bad as nails on a chalkboard and I instinctively placed my hands over my ears. I was momentarily mesmerized by the sparks that erupted from the blades, and Jim, who was chasing them. With his friends busy laughing, I made my move.

I didn't even make it out of the courtyard when Jim yelled at his buddies to grab me. A moment later, one did and held me until the others caught up. Jim's arrogant swagger had me rolling my eyes. Jeez, the drama! This guy sure liked being in the spotlight. I wondered if I'd get the chance to deck him in his smiling face before he took me down.

"You're dead," he said, as he raised his fist.

"Hey, why don't you pick on someone your own size?"

We all turned to look, to see who it was. I almost started laughing with happiness. It was Eddy and a few buddies. Eddy was known as the toughest fighter in town. He was unbeaten, and even though Jim was considerably bigger than Eddy, he wasn't about to take him on.

"Let her go," he said, with quiet malice. Jim nodded to his friends and they let me go. I wanted to run over to Eddy and throw my arms around him, but that just wouldn't be cool. "Never show fear, Montana," my dad always said. I waltzed over, copying Jim's arrogance perfectly, and stood beside Eddy.

Jim and his buddies left, and Eddy said goodnight to his friends and told me he was walking me home. Being my best buddy, he listened to the whole story without saying a word. When I was done I expected him to agree with what I had done, instead he gave me a lecture. I hated the lecture because it was almost word for word the same one Ace always gave me. "You need to control your temper, Montana, and stop getting into situations you can't get out of on your own. I won't alway be around to bail your ass out!" It was all true of course, both of them were totally right but I really hated admitting it. I finished the retelling and added that last part for Eddy's benefit, and we both broke out laughing.

    We sat chatting about stuff at school and then he left. I went back to daydreaming about Adam. The guy was so hot and it was hard not to picture myself in all sorts of different situations with him. I was sure he'd be nicer than Ace, and more understanding then even Eddy. I laughed at the image of Adam teaching me to draw, as Danny had tried so many times, and our short session always ended with me throwing my pencil at him and storming off. Okay, so maybe no personal drawing tutorials from Mr. Hot was a better choice.

    Later, just as I was nodding off to sleep, I remembered why I had gone to the movies alone that night- *to forget*. I had planned on going with my boyfriend Matthew Ross, but we'd had a fight earlier and he had roared off in his stupid Mustang. I groaned as I thought about seeing him the next morning at school. I'd stick close to my brother Alex and his band buddies, I thought, and hopefully this thing with Matt would just blow over.

Chapter 4

November 1981

Matthew Ross had been a mistake for so many reasons. Just the echo of his name resulted in an involuntary twitch that I became aware of in real time. Feeling my body meant that consciousness was near. I decided to explore that for a moment, and tentatively allowed myself to become aware of my surroundings.

At first I questioned, was I still in the land of the living? There was just a jumble of sound and noise that had no distinction and was harsh and invasive after the quietness of my silent moving pictures.

After some time, I was able to define the murmuring of voices too far off to hear clearly and the beeping and clicking of machines. If that wasn't a wake up call that I was in a hospital, the smell of disinfectant sealed it.

So Danny had saved me, damn him! But life is a choice and I don't have to ever come out of what I assumed was a coma. I could remain in a state of vegetation until they pull the plug. That thought brought me great comfort, as it was a reminder that the choice was mine to make. Now, what had I been reflecting on? Oh yeah, Matthew Ross.

April 1980

I'd woken up to a gorgeous sunny day, and leapt out of bed when I realized it was Friday. Game night and then the weekend. Two blissful days of sleeping in and doing whatever the hell I wanted.

On our walk to school I remembered Matthew, and as we turned the corner, heading to the main entrance of the school I saw him and knew he was waiting for me. Instantly my smile turned upside down. So much for my "gorgeous Friday." Beside me, Alex squeezed my hand before he and Ralph took a different entrance into the school leaving me with my "boyfriend."

As I faced Matthew, I pondered how Alex always instinctively knew what was going on with me without any verbal communication at all. We had a special bond, I knew, but he seemed more tapped into it than me.

"Hey, Montana, got a minute?" Matthew asked.

"Like no, Matt, I have class in a minute. Maybe after school."

He looked pissed off, but I wanted the upper hand, so kept on walking and left him to stew for the next five hours. I knew I was being a jerk, but with the way I was wired, stopping to dance for a puppeteer wanting to pull my strings wasn't happening. Classes went all too quickly. I left my locker, headed downstairs, walked out the main door and almost walked right into, yes, you got it, Matt.

"Hello, Matthew," I said, using a tone that imparted that I was pissed and he was taking up my valuable time.

"Are you ready to talk?" he asked.

"I guess so," I answered with a touch of sulkiness in my voice. "But I have to be back at the school for cheerleading practice before the game at 7:00."

Eddy was walking by at that precise moment, so I wished him good luck in the game and told him to kick some Tupper butt. He sent me a wink as I got into Matt's car. "Call Me" by Blondie was playing. I turned it up thinking of Adam, and Matt turned it off.

We drove in silence over the Burrard Bridge and along Jericho Beach and Spanish Banks. Finally, he parked by a trail leading into the bushes at the University of British Columbia. Matt picked his way down a path that leveled out about twenty feet down and motioned for me to join him on a fallen tree.

As soon as we sat he whipped out a joint and lit it up. I watched in annoyance as he knew I didn't want any but apparently, he needed a hit just to talk to me.

"So, what's up?" I finally asked, breaking the irritating silence.

"You were pretty mad yesterday," he replied.

"I'm still mad. You were a real jerk yesterday," I said back, with ice in my voice.

"You're right. I was a real jerk yesterday."

That was not the reaction I was expecting.

"I spoke with Patrick last night," he continued. "And told him what happened. He said, "she's right and you're wrong, so apologize to her.""

Patrick Woods was an ex-boyfriend, and one I considered a friend. He was best friends with Matt, and very good friends with Eddy, and to a lesser extent, my brother Danny. It was Pat who'd convinced me to give Matt a shot. That had been three months ago.

Our dating had been more posturing than real. We pretty much ignored each other at school and he was a ride and an easy access to rum on the weekends. He wasn't exactly boyfriend material but until last night, our casual dating hadn't really mattered all that much. My decision to ditch Matt had been decided on my walk to school. I could do better than yo-yo dating a guy who yes had a thing for me but was skating along edges that didn't jive with who I was. Besides, we hadn't had fun for weeks now, so it was bye-bye time. "Matt, I appreciate the apology. It wasn't all you, so I'm sorry too, okay?"

He smiled in response... great. This ditching thing was getting harder by the moment.

"Uh, Matt, I have to tell you something."

"If this is about the guy who picked you up last night and took you home, don't bother. I know all about it, and don't worry, Mo, I'm not mad. I forgive you."

My jaw dropped, and Matt was giving me that Cheshire cat grin, you know that stupid cat in *Alice in Wonderland*? My blood began to boil. I mean, who the hell did this guy think he was, anyway? Was he a spy, or did he employ a spy to watch everything I did, or did Eddy say something?

He noticed me getting angry and stood up and started yelling about stupid things from the past. I knocked the stupid joint out of his hand and started yelling right back. Next thing I knew, I was on my butt on the ground and the side of my face felt like it was exploding and my ears were ringing. Matt stood above me with a shocked look on his face that quickly changed to horror and then guilt.

"Mo, I am so sorry. Oh, God, I don't know why I did that. We better go and get some ice. Your face is swelling already."

"Swelling," I said in a scathing voice. "Matt, screw you, I don't want to hear from you ever again!"

"Wait, Montana..."

But I didn't wait; I kept walking up the trail, angry and in shock. He had hit me, and not a light slap either, a full-blown, knocked me to the ground punch! I felt the swelling increase as I walked to the nearest gas station at Alma and 6th, a good two miles from where we'd parked.

I asked for the bathroom key, the station clerk gave me a pitying look as he handed over the key, asking me if I was okay.

God! I hated people's sympathy! It was like nails on a chalkboard. I'm tough, afterall. West End raised, jock, cheerleader, with three controlling brothers, you know, like, I can handle myself. I surveyed the damage in the mirror. From my nose down, the colour was purple, and my lip was cut and swollen. No wonder I got those looks. How embarrassing.

There was no way I could go home. If Danny or Ace saw me, they would flip. I knew I could call Chrissie and get her to meet me and do one of her famous makeup jobs. Thank God for girlfriends, I thought as I called her up from the station payphone.

"Chrissie, it's me, Mo. Listen, I can't get into it right now, but I need you to do me a favour. Go to my house and get my cheerleading gear and meet me at the school."

"Mo, are you okay? What's going on, where are you?"

"Honestly, Chrissie, I don't know if I'm okay. I'm still in shock. Matt punched me pretty hard, and right now I'm at a gas station at Alma and 6th, and I have a long way to walk to get to the Burrard Bridge. I'm just praying I get to the school by 5:00 for practice. Oh hey, and listen up, I need you to bring all the makeup you have as you're going to be covering up the damage for me."

I hung up the phone and headed down to Fourth Avenue and along Fourth for the bridge. I was starting to come down from my anger high and was now feeling tired, sore, and emotionally empty. This was not the time to analyze that last one, it was time to come up with a story, and one everyone would buy, including my brothers.

I contemplated a few scenarios as I walked the bridge. As I neared the other side, I caught sight of Chrissie and Eddy. Damn! Obviously, she had run into him while grabbing my gear, and for whatever reason, he had not bought whatever excuse she had given him. I watched their faces as I neared them, looking for the same reaction that the passer-byers had given me -*Sympathy*. Yuck!

Eddy's expression morphed from shock to anger, while Chrissie's went from shock to worry. They were my best friends and I knew I'd be okay.

Chrissie ran over and threw her arms around me, "Mo, are you okay? You look awful!"

"Actually, I feel like shit. My entire head is pounding, and with each step I take, the pressure builds in my face. A constant reminder of what just happened."

Eddy didn't say a word as he led us off the bridge to Sunset Beach so we could sit and let me rest for a bit—and interrogate me, of course. Did I mention that Eddy wanted to be a cop when he grew up? Well, I like to take credit for giving him the best training any young man could ask for. We sat down, and I related the story from beginning to end to the two of them. I also mentioned that I needed their help with a cover-up story. Eddy was not pleased with the idea of a cover-up story; he was all for the truth.

He knew what Matt had done was out of character. He also knew that Ace wouldn't ask any questions; he would either kill Matt or send him to the hospital.

"Montana, I'm concerned that this has really nothing to do with protecting Matt. This is your way of protecting yourself and avoiding confrontation. Besides, I'm not at all convinced that I shouldn't hunt him down myself for what he did."

In response, I gave him my most pathetic, begging look, and he finally agreed to help me and let it go at that. I gave him a big hug, and the three of us headed off to the school. Chrissie had taken a few make-up courses and did a great job covering up the damage to my face, although the lip on the side with the cut was a challenge as it was swollen, and covered it looked like I'd been stung by a bee. I would keep my distance from anyone I knew, and from the bleachers where my brothers would be sitting, the damage to my face would not be noticed.

Just before the game, Chrissie ran over to the store and got me some Tylenol to ease the pain and all was ready. At halftime, Eddy approached me and told me the cover-up story I would be telling my brothers and anyone else who asked.

"You and Matt were in the UBC woods like you said, but on the way back to the car, you guys were jumped by a small gang that you didn't recognize. You two ran because you were outnumbered, and when you got to the car, Matt leaned across to throw the door open for you just as you were leaning down to open it. *Wham*, the door hit you in the face, and you were knocked out.

Matt threw you in the car and drove you to Chrissie where she helped you with your wounds, and Matt went back to see if he could find the guys, which explains his absence tonight."

This was one of the many reasons I loved Eddy. "Awesome story, Eddy, but what if Matt spills the real story?" I asked.

"Already taken care of, Mo. I phoned Pat, and he's driving in from Abbotsford tonight to see Matt and talk to him in person. Pat feels bad, Mo. He wants to see you with his own eyes to make sure you're okay. I guess he feels responsible as he talked you into dating Matt in the first place."

"Pat knows I want no trouble. Right, Eddy? I mean he won't do anything, will he?"

"He'll respect your wishes, Mo. It's all good."

Well, thank God that part was done. Now all I had to do was convince my brothers of the story, and then everything would be cool.

After the game, Eddy, I, and my three brothers went to Olympia Pizza. I relayed the entire story just as Eddy had laid it out. Ace and Danny bought it and even wanted to hook up with Matt and help him track the guys who jumped us.

Eddy convinced them not to bother, as he felt Matt was wasting his time, as neither Matt nor I got a look at any of the gang members. Alex gave me a look that said he knew I was lying but said nothing. I would have to give him the real story at some point when we were alone.

Ace laid into me about not coming home after it happened, but I rationalized that it would have done me no good, as he had been at school and then work, and Dan had been at an art thing, and Alex was having band practice.

Chrissie was the logical choice, as she was home and could help. Ace accepted that explanation and informed me he was taking me to the doctor in the morning to make sure I didn't have a concussion or anything serious.

The next day, Ace and I received some strange looks from both the doctor and his receptionist. They probably thought he beat me, but I got a clean bill and they also accepted my story. I was given the order to rest the rest of the morning and not to do anything strenuous for a few days.

When I showed up at school in the afternoon, with no makeup on. There was no point as the rumours had already been spread about me and Matt and the gang attack.

I looked pretty cool to everyone but my friends who probably suspected that my story was bullshit but no one would call me out on it. To the rest of the school, my popularity and reputation for being a badass strengthened. I guess sometimes good things could happen even when they started off bad.

The next day I did come clean with Alex on a walk around Lost Lagoon. He agreed with me that Ace would have seriously harmed or even killed Matt, so all in all, it was a good call. He'd never liked me with Matt, anyhow; he said Matt walked a dangerous line and that eventually, I would have been caught up in his extra-curricular activities. He said the last thing I needed was to be stuck in yet another place that provided opportunities for me to make bad choices.

I laughed at Alex's impersonation of our eldest brother, and punched him playfully in the arm. He had asked who my next victim was to be, but I didn't answer.

I didn't want to date anyone, but at the same time, my mind kept going back to Adam. My dreamy, artistic, philanthropist poet from the other side of town. The only son of a rich construction mogul, I'd heard from Danny. It was clear that Mr. Rich and Sexy, four years my senior, wouldn't be interested, but a girl could dream, right? Alex caught the dreamy smile on my face and gave me a nudge... my sensitive brother picked up on my thoughts, and we both laughed. We walked in silence as we made our way home. Enjoying our quiet connection.

It was time for band practice and my night for cooking dinner. I was in the mood for making a dining experience. I got out mom's cookbook and the dishes she'd used for special occasions. Basically, going all out to my brothers amazement. We sat around the dinner table and joked for hours. It was the first time in a long time that the four of us just hung out and enjoyed each other's company. I, for one, stored it in my memory bank, to use at a later date in a song or poem.

Whether it is fear or despair or, as in my case, pain.

Chapter 5

November 1981

Consciousness must have momentarily surfaced, because I was aware of someone calling my name in real time. It sounded as if from a great distance or like the sound in a canyon reverberating back when someone yelled. I knew the voice but couldn't place it, and didn't want to waste any time trying to. I was impatient to get back to the movie of my life. The process allowed me to see my life as a distant observer. All the details—things I remembered and things I knew I'd missed. I was impatient for more, that part of me hadn't changed. I'd always been impatient and now was no different. I needed to know how my movie ended.

Fall 1980

"Hey everyone, have you met the new kid yet?" Otter asked, as he joined the crew outside on the grass for our school lunch break. A few weeks had passed since my run in with Matt and a new kid in town was just what we needed to break up the monotony of school and gigs. Well the monotony for me, everyone else was fine with how things were.

I'd used the break up as an opportunity to dig deep and write a whole new playlist of songs for the band to learn. Although this new round of songs was a lot like romance, it made little to no sense but it wasn't about that, it was about how you felt when you were going through it. "Wings" had come out with a song in the late 70's called Silly Love Songs. It was a hit. Need I say more?

"Who is he?" Alex yelled from the grass where Dillon had him in a headlock. Boys, I thought, and shook my head.

"Not a him, Alex, a her—a really cute her. I invited her to come out and meet you guys, so be nice," he said, looking at me when he said it. Otter gave us the scoop on Mercedes. She had just transferred from some school in Abbotsford, and her locker was right beside his, which is why he knew of her already.

Just then, a very attractive, Jamaican-looking girl walked out and shyly made her way over to Otter, who was beaming with delight and looking like a total idiot.

"Everyone, this is Mercedes."

"Oh please," she piped up. "Mercy for short. Mercedes is too long of a name to be saying, so Mercy would be great."

We took turns introducing ourselves, but when she met Alex, her eyes lingered for a while, sizing him up and obviously liking what she saw. Unfortunately, Otter noticed also.

"Alex and Montana are twins," he said, directing her focus from Alex to me.

Like I was going to help him, not! Ah, what the hell. I'd try and help the poor love-struck sap. "Yeah, and we have two older brothers also, Ace and Danny," I tossed in more Stanfords just to be helpful.

"Mmm," she mumbled. "Must be good-looking if you two look like them."

Epic fail on my part. Alex blushed and I nudged Chrissie to see if she noticed. Alex never blushed, which meant he must have felt an attraction for her. I hoped for Otter's sake that Alex wouldn't want to date Mercy. Otter couldn't take his eyes off her. I wanted to keep an eye on the "new girl," and control what could become a nasty triangle and have Chrissie invite us girls over after school to hang out.

I watched Mercy and she seemed like a cool chick. She was into the same stuff as us. She loved classic rock: ACDC, The Who, The Rolling Stones. Her favourite actor was Matt Dillon, and her favourite movie *Little Darlings*, which Matt Dillon starred in.

Her family had moved from Abbotsford, because her parents had separated and her mom had gotten a job in the city. Her dad had moved to North Vancouver.

They lived close enough that Mercedes could visit her dad whenever she wanted. She seemed to check out okay and jive with our group, so we invited her to join us down at Second Beach that weekend for a bonfire party.

Chapter 6

November 1981

Mercedes, that name made me shudder. She had been the cause of so much trouble and in my gut I knew that if I lived she would continue to be a thorn in my side.

Fall 1980

Friday arrived and it was Dillon's turn to find some rando to go into the liquor store for us and get the rum for our beach party. Alex, Otter, Ralph, and I went to 7-11 to get the Big Gulps filled with coke for our mix. Dillon had managed to sweet talk someone into getting us the goods and when we arrived at our favourite section of Second Beach, I divvied up the rum and cokes to everyone while the guys collected driftwood for our fire.

We used Big Gulp cups for two reasons. 1) the cops patrolled the beaches and with those cups they never suspected us of drinking booze. 2) Sometimes Eddy would come by with Danny, who couldn't know we were drinking because for most of us, 'legal drinking age' seemed as far in the future as an episode of Star Trek.

We hadn't been there long when Mercy pulled out a joint and lit up. That was a bit of a shock, as none of us had tried drugs to my knowledge, with the exception of Matt who we never included in our core parties anyway. Although no one said anything, you could feel the tension. She held out the doobie to us all to see if anyone else wanted any.

"You know, Mercy," I said, "we don't do drugs. They're for losers, but you go ahead, we'll watch." Not well said, but I wanted to make my point and hopefully get her to stop.

"I would have never taken you for a chicken, Montana. You like everyone to think you're a badass, but that's okay, you have it your way. Just sit there like a good little girl and watch the real badass."

All eyes were on me. I had a reputation for being tough, and not many people would talk to me like that. I wanted to beat the crap out of her and make her swallow her words. I looked at Alex, and he shook his head no—he knew what was going on in my mind. But clearly the gauntlet had been thrown, and I had to do something.

"Okay, Mercy. I'll tell you what, hotshot, you drink down what's left in your cup in one minute flat, and I will smoke your joint with you. Deal?"

Mercy picked up her cup, took off the lid and showed everyone how much was left for her to down. The cups were huge, and hers was two thirds full. I thought there was no way she could do it.

She threw her lid down and chugged. Otter was the timer to make sure she didn't cheat. In fifty seconds she had done it. I hated to admit I was impressed, but I was. The girl had a gut of steel!

My turn was next. She relit the joint and passed it to me.

I took a small toke, as I didn't want to look like a total amateur by inhaling too much and coughing. No one said a word, but watched us as we passed it back and forth between us until it was gone. I wanted to congratulate myself on performing well, but as soon as we finished I was thirsty but my cup was empty. Ralph was beside me, and I reached for his cup, chugging down what was left.

Later, when it was time to leave, I attempted to stand and ended up toppling over Ralph. I was laughing so hard I couldn't get up, and remained on Ralph's lap until Alex intervened and helped me stand. I stood, swaying in Alex's grasp. When he let go, I promptly fell back into Ralph's lap. I was feeling brave and put my arms around him. He put his arms around me and smiled, looking amused at my silly, drunken antics.

"Gee, Ralph," I said. "Did I ever tell you that you're really cute? And I like the way you play the skins, too."

"Uh-oh, Alex, Mo is pissed. What are we going to do with her?" Ralph asked with a huge grin, not looking at all as concerned as his words had implied.

"She could stay at my house," Mercy said. I looked at her as she spoke, and I swear on my life, the girl had a demonic expression on her face. It totally freaked me out. I shivered and sent Alex a pleading look. He thanked Mercy for her offer, but said he had another plan in mind.

I grinned at Ralph, "I could always spend the night at your house, Masters," and keeled over with laughter imagining me and him sharing a bed. I was higher than a kite but I swore a look of want came and went before the two of them stood and between them kept me steady.

"I should let Mercy have you," Alex whispered in my ear. "Now behave yourself. I'm taking you to Eddy's. You can sleep in the spare room."

When we arrived at Eddy's, he took one look at me, picked me up, and carried me into the spare room in the garage where he dumped me on the bed and left. He showed up a few minutes later with water and a bucket. He rubbed my back as I fell asleep, and the next thing I knew, it was morning and Alex was shaking me awake. He was just going home from Ralph's and figured he better get me home before the guys asked too many questions.

Ace and Danny were still asleep when we arrived. Alex and I went to the kitchen and I sat in silence drinking coffee while watching him make breakfast for everyone. I was way too hungover for anything else. The guys must have smelled the food, as they came in just as Alex was serving up plates filled with Millie's special pancakes, a recipe from mom's cookbook, and crispy bacon, my favourite.

Ace was cheerful for a change, trading in his constant frown for a curling up of his lip that was rare to see. Under normal circumstances I would have been happy to see him happy, but feeling like I did, I just wanted to tell him off so I could nurse my hangover in peace. Ace chatted amicably about everything under the sun and by some miracle of god I managed to keep my mouth shut until breakfast was almost done. Finally I caved and asked what he was so friggin' happy about, Ace answered that he had gone on a date last night. That got our attention, as he hadn't dated in at least two years.

"With who?" the three of us asked simultaneously.

"A freshman named Kristine. Pete, Dillon's older brother, knows her and introduced us last week, so I asked her out and she said yes. Last night was our first date."

"First?" I asked sullenly. "So, you're going out again?"

"I want details," Danny said.

"No way," Ace answered as he grabbed the pillow from behind his back and threw it at Danny.

The siblings all played by one rule, whoever threw a pillow signaled the rest that it was game on.

"Attack!" Alex yelled.

The chase was on. Ace got up and ran to the living room with the three of us in hot pursuit. I made a detour to the bathroom for water guns and tossed one to Alex as I ran back in the room. Ace had been sitting in a big chair when Alex and Danny tackled him, they all went right over.

"Quick, Mo, shoot him!" Alex yelled, and he and Danny worked to keep Ace down on the ground. We were all laughing so much it was hard to be accurate. I finally just sat on Ace's chest and shot away until my water ran out. The house became a giant Slip 'N Slide as I broke away to reload and Alex and I continued shooting back and forth, the three of us going after Ace and running when he would come after us.

By the time we had played ourselves out and cleaned up, it was lunch time and we were all starving. We talked Ace into taking us to McDonald's for lunch. Not my favourite, but we hadn't been there together since forever, so I kept my mouth shut as we walked over to Robson and Bidwell Street to the McDonald's.

Pat, Eddy and Matt were there and invited us to sit with them. Matt and I hadn't spoken a word to each other since that day in the woods weeks earlier.

We avoided eye contact, but other than that, everything was good. When lunch was over, we decided to join the guys for a game of basketball at Lord Roberts.

Matt wanted to talk, so we hung back and let the others go ahead of us.

"Montana, I want to apologize for what happened that day in the woods. It has been bothering me ever since and I wanted to ask, would you forgive me?"

I was processing that when next he said, "Listen, I need to tell Ace the truth about what happened, and if he beats me up or worse, I accept that."

"Are you insane?" I almost yelled as I stopped walking and looked at him. "You can't do that. There's more at risk than just your ass, you know. I lied to them to protect you, and Eddy and Pat, your buddies, covered up for you. Ace will look at that as a betrayal and you'll put a wall between him and the guys."

He was silent and looked thoughtful as he processed what I'd said. "Mo, I really appreciate what you and the guys did, but it's wrong. I can't look Dan in the eyes, and we've been friends since we were little kids. Also, my relationship with both Eddy and Pat is not the same, and whenever I see Ace, I just feel guilty. It's an ugly secret that I can't live with anymore. Seeing you for days with those bruises and cuts on your face ate away at me, and I have to come clean. I hope when I explain it, your brothers will see that you were only trying to do the right thing, and now it's my turn to do the same. I'm sorry for what that means for you, but that's my decision."

His decision. It sounded more like a *him* problem that he was laying at my feet. Had I known this idiot would ruin a perfectly good cover up, I would have come clean right from the start. Would I have, though? It was hard to remember now why it seemed so important at the time to keep the truth to the few who would get it, and then I remembered, because yes, while Ace would definitely hurt him and he deserved it, the entire thing put me at the front of a messy, embarrassing situation. I didn't like those situations and usually did anything in my power to avoid the fallout afterward, like Eddy was always telling me.

We had arrived at the basketball court, and my mind was doing overtime as I tried to find a way out of what was about to happen. Ace was going to be so pissed off at me. He would blame me, and as the disciplinarian in our house, he was never lenient when it came to lying.

"Ace, Danny," Matt said, "could I talk with you two for a minute? In fact, I would love to tell you all, so could we delay the game for a moment? I have something to say. Before I begin, I ask that you take it easy on Montana. She was just trying to protect me, and although I appreciate it, I need to come clean on some things."

I felt my cheeks burning and kept my eyes down as Matt told the real story of what happened in the woods that day. He never mentioned Eddy or Pat, which I was grateful for. At the end of the story I could feel all eyes on me and, if possible, my cheeks burned even brighter.

"Montana, look at me," Ace said.

Oh God, I felt like crawling under a rock. I looked up into Ace's eyes and was relieved to see he didn't look as angry as I thought he would.

"Montana, is everything Matt said correct? If there's anything to add, you better tell me now, as this will be your only chance. Do you understand?"

"Yes, I understand," I replied with a gulp. Ace's expression morphed into the don't-mess-with-me look or you won't sit comfortably for a week. I looked to Eddy to seek permission to tell the rest of the tale, and he nodded his head, so I told what Matt didn't know. When I finished my tale, Ace looked at Matt and thanked him for having the guts to come clean and asked him why he had.

"Truth is, Ace, I felt really bad about the whole thing; Mo covering for me was eating me alive. Also, I didn't want Mo to think that every time something goes wrong she needs to cover for people to keep them from their just punishment."

Ace digested that as the rest of us stood waiting for what he would decide would be a just punishment.

"Honestly, Matt, Montana is right. At the time, you would have landed in the hospital. I'm still pissed that you hit my sister, and normally I would do you in just for that. However, you've impressed me by being responsible for your actions. You've put some thought into this. I'm going to deck you the same way you decked her, and then we can shake hands and put this whole thing behind us."

I was elated everything was going to be okay. Matt braced himself and Ace took his swing. Matt ended up on his ass but not knocked out. He stood up moments later and they shook hands. Ace then turned his focus on me next.

"Mo, you and I have some talking to do. I'm disappointed with you right now, and I don't even feel like I know you anymore." He looked at Dan pointedly while saying, "I'm sure Dan has some things he wishes to say, as well." Danny nodded in agreement, and with that, the four of us headed for home.

What a brutal day it turned out to be. The two of them tag-teamed their lecturing to me for hours, or so it seemed, about trust and being honest no matter what. In the end, it was decided that I was grounded for two weeks for holding back what they both considered to be a huge truth. Funny how neither of them considered how I felt about it as I was the victim after all. Thank goodness little white lies were not mentioned because no way could I have made a promise not to tell them. I got the point, however, and made a silent oath to be on my best behavior... for a while at least.

Chapter 7

November 1981

I'd promised to behave, to tell my brother everything, but I'd been so naive in thinking I was capable of sharing the larger issues. I kept secrets that made keeping a dick like Matt safe look juvenile at best. It was the beginning of what brought me to the point of watching my life replay like a movie.

Fall 1980

I didn't know what to say to Mercy when I got home from school and there she was, sitting on my porch. Rumours about our beach party had spread quickly around school, and not all of them shone on me favorably. It was hard to tell if she was here to gloat or to be my friend, but I had nothing to lose by inviting her in.

"Montana, I wanted to apologize to you for that night at the beach. I guess I was feeling a bit insecure being the new kid, and I wanted to impress everyone. It was stupid, though, 'cause there you were being a friend to me, and I was being a bitch."

That was not what I expected at all, and wondered if maybe it had been the drugs that made me see her demon face. She seemed sincere in her apology and decided our burgeoning friendship was with a do-over.

"I only have five days left of my confinement." I rolled my eyes.

Mercy laughed. "In plenty of time for the next party?"

"Absolutely! No contests this time though."

"Scouts honor," she said and crossed herself.

"The guys just started practice, wanna go to the garage and watch them?"

"Sure, that sounds like fun, she answered enthusiastically. I was happy to have our issue dealt with and led her to the garage. Otter noticed her first and gave her a wink. I don't think she saw it, as she was busy checking out Alex, who was in the middle of a guitar solo. Ugh! So much for no issues between us. I was pretty sure when I told her to back off my brother we'd be at loggerheads. Mercy didn't like being told anything and I was the definitive leader in our circle of friends and would always speak my mind when it came to them, especially my twin.

Chapter 8

November 1981

Mercy, what an evil girl she would turn out to be, but as Adam always says, the truth always comes out eventually. Adam...Halloween 1980 flashed with images of costumes and him dressed as Zorro. He'd looked like a sexy man amongst a bunch of children. I must have given an outward indication of consciousness, because I felt someone squeeze my hand. Next, I heard words being whispered in my ear. It was Ace and he sounded so sad, and so far away. I wanted to comfort him, but the pictures were pulling me back.

October 31, 1980

It was Halloween and our crew was in a festive mood. Alex and the guys were about to play their biggest gig to date at the local community centre. They played a lot of places for free to build up their fan base and it was finally paying off.

I'd negotiated the deal and was excited as they were about playing in our local centre and 300.00 bucks was pretty good pay for a group of teenagers. I received 10% as the booking agent which I looked at as rum funds for our beach parties.

Hundreds of tickets had been sold, and our excitement was contagious. Finally the locals would see Behind Blue Eyes play and we fully anticipated getting a few gigs from the large turnout. Cash prizes were being awarded for best costume, as well as for best dancers, singles and couples.

Mercedes and I had grown closer, and she and I had been practicing some moves together hoping to win in the best dancers category. Ace was taking his new girlfriend—well, he wasn't calling her that yet, but we all knew that Kristine was his new girlfriend, first one since high school.

Ace had always said that between work, school and us, there wasn't time for women. For him to spend so much of what little free time he had with her, showed that he really liked her. I was happy, not happy for him. On the one hand, it benefited me as he was less controlling, on the other, I rarely saw him these days.

Alex had already been at the centre for hours, doing sound checks and making sure everything was perfect. I had been warned earlier that day to keep cool and to stay close to my chaperone, Danny. It was my first night out since being grounded.

The place was packed when we arrived. There were some really cool costumes. Ace and Kristine came as Lancelot and Guinevere, and won for best couples costume. Like bite me! To me they just looked sappy. Danny and the guys came as greasers from the 1960s, and the band members dressed up like convicts. I went as a bellydancer, Chrissie came as a hooker, and Mercy came as Helen of Troy; she was stunning.

In Greek mythology, Helen falls in love with the wrong guy (Paris) and all hell breaks loose. I couldn't help but feel perhaps the outfit was a message to Alex. Anyway, you should have heard the catcalls and whistles as we walked from my house to the community centre. It was too funny, but we girls glowed from all the praise.

Otter was the first to notice us from the stage. Alex didn't look over until Otter screwed up the music, and Alex looked around to find out what happened and followed his sight line to us. I watched as his eyes roved from me to Mercy and landed on Chrissie where they stayed. He seemed mesmerized. I almost laughed aloud when I looked over and saw the expression on Mercy's face. Boy was she angry! Chrissie, however, was positively glowing with the attention as others turned to see what had Alex's attention. She'd stolen the limelight from Mercy without even trying.

"Mercy, is there something wrong?"

"Nothing," she said, but the expression on her face said otherwise.

Mercy excused herself and went closer to the stage. I lost sight of her and turned my attention to Chrissie.

"Is there something going on between you and my brother?" I had to ask.

She grinned.

"To be honest, I've had a crush on Alex since the third grade."

I was surprised. I had never noticed her checking him out or vice versa. I finally mustered, "I'm your best friend. Why didn't you tell me?"

"I didn't think he would like me the same way I liked him, so it seemed pointless to tell you or anyone else. And if I had told you, you would have set us up. He would have felt obligated to date me because of being your best friend, and I just wanted him to like me without any interference."

She was right, of course. That's exactly what I would have done. She knew me too well, I chuckled to myself. I looked at Alex, and watched him stare at her. There was definitely something there and she, as I already said, was glowing. I decided to leave the two to ogle at each other in relative peace and went in search of Mercy.

I found her at the punch bowl. "It's spiked," she said, handing me a glass. We slipped outside for some air. "Mercy," I began, "I have a feeling that you have a thing for my brother Alex." Before I could say more, her attitude changed, and all of the sudden the evilness at the beach I'd seen didn't seem like a case of being high. Her voice was coy when she responded like she was playing apart. Maybe she had a split personality disorder.

"Why, Montana, I don't know what you're talking about." She batted her eyes at me. This was getting me nowhere except frustrated. I decided to change tactics.

"Mercy, what do you think of Otter?"

"Oh, he's fine I guess, if you are attracted to that kind of guy. Why, Montana, do you like him?"

This was ridiculous; she knew perfectly well I didn't. I decided to just be blunt and cut through her crap. "Fair warning, Alex is off the market."

"Since when?"

"Since I said so, duh!" She shrugged and went back inside. I decided to go and calm down at the punch bowl and have another glass or two… what the hell, maybe more, a lot more. I was facing the entrance when Zorro walked in. I paused the glass halfway to my mouth and stoop gaping at the hottest male I'd ever seen. What I wouldn't give to slip the mask down and see who was underneath. I wasn't the only girl standing looking stupefied as he strode into the room.

I wracked my brain trying to think of anyone I knew that could look that good in that costume but the only one who came to mind was Adam. Was he supposed to becoming to the dance? Danny never said anything about him joining us. Strangely, Zorro noticed me and headed right over to the punch bowl where I stood.

"Hi, Montana, love the costume. You look really sexy in it."

Holy crap, it was Adam: Adam was Zorro. "Um, Adam, wow, you're Zorro… you look, um, really good also," I said blushing furiously. "Did you come with anyone?" I asked.

"I came by myself, but I'm supposed to be linking up with Danny and his buddies. Any idea where they are?"

Did I ever, and rolled my eyes. The dorks had been in the punch and sneaking outside for shots. They were now over on the other side of the room wrestling like little boys. I told

Adam, and he just laughed and had me lead the way. When we linked with the guys, Danny had Pat down in a choke hold.

He stood up when he noticed us and introduced Adam to the guys. He didn't ask how I knew Adam, which I thought odd, but then again, he had a good buzz on. Maybe he just overlooked the fact that Adam and I didn't know each other. At least as far as Danny was concerned, we didn't know each other.

Eddy gave me a wink, however. He must have recognized Adam as being the hot guy in the hot car that had dropped me off at the corner that night of the movies.

"Montana, don't have any punch. Go to the counter instead, if you get thirsty."

"Why is that, Dan?" I grinned. "Afraid I'm gonna get a sugar high?"

"No, smarty pants, someone has spiked the punch and I don't need you getting drunk."

"No! Someone spiked the punch bowl, that's awful," I replied, in mock indignation.

Beside me Adam grinned but didn't out me.

"Besides," Danny added, "Ace would kill us both if I let you get drunk."

"I doubt it," I retorted. "I mean, look at the guy. He wouldn't notice if the ceiling caved in and fell on his head. He's all eyes for Kristine." As one, several heads turned and looked at where I was pointing. One look at Ace looking all twitterpated had them howling.

A few minor incidents happened throughout the rest of the evening, including one with Mercy. She decided to ignore my advice regarding Alex. While I was busy with Adam, she told Chrissie that Alex liked her, and that they were an item. I cleared it up with Chrissie, but when I went to find Mercy to chew her out for lying and hurting Chrissie's feelings, she was gone.

I knew I'd see her later at the beach party, and would confront her then.

Zorro, the convicts, the greasers and I went to Olympia Pizza and had a great time. Danny and Pat were pretty loaded from the punch, and they kept throwing sugar packets at each other. Adam decided to join in and put the little creamers on my head and tossed a few at Danny. One accidentally landed on Matt and it exploded, covering his head in cream. We were all laughing when the waitress arrived with the pizzas.

We settled down long enough to stuff our faces. I saved my crusts so I could throw them. I chucked one at Pat, who in turn tried to catch it in his mouth. Then Danny and Matt tried to catch crusts simultaneously. The rest of us did seagull impersonations and were getting pretty loud when, to my surprise, Mercy walked in. She had her fake smile pasted on as she walked over to us and said hello.

"Matt invited me," she said as she slid onto Matt's lap. Then she looked straight at me and said, "Oh, didn't you know?" and she gave me that coy Cheshire cat grin that Matt was so good at. I was beginning to really hate that damn look.

Well, I had to give her credit. She worked fast. She obviously thought Matt was a worthier target than Otter. Matt and I had been over for a while, and although Mercy came along after he and I had split, going out with a "friend's" ex was just not cool. Matt seemed uncomfortable. Maybe he picked up my vibe... as he stood up rather abruptly, almost dumping Mercy on the floor. It was time to go, he said. At the door, Mercy turned and called out, "I guess we'll see you later at the beach party."

What a cow. She had done that on purpose. She knew Danny didn't know about the party. I was supposed to go home, and then I was going to sneak out later. Damn! Now I would have to fess up.

"You can count on it," I said back in my iciest voice.

"Montana," Danny said. "What party is she talking about?"

Eddy quickly stepped in and filled Danny in on the party. Everything was in motion for tonight. Everyone would keep quiet regarding the alcohol, and hopefully Danny would never guess. In true West End tradition, we bought Big Gulps so no one would know we were drinking. Teens had been doing this for years, as the cops were frequent visitors to the beach. Having no "bottles" gave them nothing to suspect, so they left us in peace.

We arrived at the beach and Chrissie and Kim were already there. Alex and I went off to dump our mickey of rum into our Big Gulp cups. Adam strolled by as we were dumping in the rum. I held a finger to my lips in a *shhhhh* fashion and he just grinned and kept on walking. I laughed and went back to the pouring. When we were done, we put our lids on, tossed the mickey into a donation pile for the bums, and went to join the party.

We sat in a circle formation, and I had Adam on one side of me and Alex on the other, with Chrissie beside him. Across from us were Matt and Mercy. I was able to ignore Mercy for the most part, and enjoy Adam's company. We discussed literature and art, two of my favourite topics. Kind of weird actually, as most kids wouldn't consider it cool.

Because Danny was in art school, I knew a lot from him. Our mother had painted, sung and danced. Alex played guitar, bass guitar and sang. I danced and wrote poetry and music. Danny knew and could do all art mediums. And Ace was in school for business and architecture. Man, Ace could talk for hours about architecture, old and new. He clearly had a passion for art, but more from a business perspective than from an artistic viewpoint although he had an amazing eye without really being aware of it. Collectively, we were a family of artists.

It became obvious throughout the evening that Adam and I had many interests in common. Adam shared some of his goals and plans for his future with me. He was the first guy I had spent time with, other than my brothers and Eddy, who had plans for the future. During our talk, I often glanced at the others, and everytime found Matt staring at me and Mercy giving sidelong glances to Alex.

She seemed to cater to Matt only when she noticed Alex or Otter watching her. The rest of the time she ignored Matt. As Adam hadn't known any of the other partygoers prior to the party, I filled him in on who was who and what they meant to me.

I told him a little about me and Matt, my friendship with Eddy, and the budding romance between my brother Alex and Chrissie. When I told him about my encounters with Mercy earlier in the evening, he said it explained why she kept looking over and glaring at me.

"She's glaring at me, really?" And as I shifted my focus to her, I saw that look again. That horrible evil look I had seen that first time we had been at the beach together. Adam saw it, too.

"Montana," Adam said, "you should be careful of her. She is the kind of person who would sell her mother for twenty dollars. She's loyal to the highest bidder, and I see nothing but trouble coming from a friendship with her." I agreed and promised to take his warning to heart.

Not long after that observation, Mercy and Matt left. The night seemed to become more fun after they'd gone, as everyone broke from their little conversations and joked and reminisced for the rest of the evening.

We finished our drinks at the stroke of midnight… weird… and decided to call it a night. Adam left with a promise to call "yeah, right", and Eddy, Danny, Alex, Chrissie and I headed back to our house. As we walked, I suggested to Danny he invite Adam over to hang out.

"Montana, I know you two are really attracted to each other and seem to have this cool connection, but don't get your hopes up. Adam has a silver spoon in his mouth and is an only child. I can't see his parents being excited about him dating a girl four years younger than him, with a chip the size of Iceland on her shoulder, and a mouth that won't quit," Danny said.

I decided to change the topic, as I had no intention of removing Adam as a future potential boyfriend. Alex was right; when I wanted something or someone, I dug in and was capable of playing the long game to get what I wanted.

When we arrived, we found a note on the table from Ace. He and Kristine had decided to go stateside for the night and said he would be home by lunch the next day. Yahoo, I thought, sneaking out for the rest of the night would be a cakewalk.

Eddy and Danny sat down in the kitchen to play poker. Alex and Chrissie disappeared into Alex's room, so I took the opportunity to say I was turning in for the night. As soon as the door to my room was shut, I was out the window. Freedom felt good, I thought, as I headed down the road looking for adventure.

Chapter 9

November 1981

The dark called to me then, like it did now, offering opportunities to be real, and if you were really lucky, expose things that the light never touched.

Fall 1980

I decided to walk down Denman Street toward the community centre and see if anyone was still hanging out after the dance. I saw a lot of kids, and said hi to many, but didn't see anything to hold my interest so I kept moving. I was just rounding the corner by the ice rink when I heard a name I recognized.

"What are you going to do, Mercy? Mess with Chrissie just to spite Montana and her brother? The Matt thing should have pissed her off. Why are you going after her best friend and twin?"

I was curious myself to hear what the response would be to that question, so I inched up closer and kept to the bushes to listen in.

"Isn't it obvious? I will take Alex for myself, oust Montana as the leader of the pack, and take over. She's so overconfident in herself and her position as leader, by the time she figures it out, her head will be spinning so fast she won't know what hit her." She said that last bit with a chuckle.

This was too much. Not only was she planning my demise, but telling it to the one group of people I'd labeled them as enemies a long time ago, and considered them as dirty players and not to be trusted. Who is Mercy, the friggin' Antichrist or something? I was just about to break cover and beat the crap out of Mercy when I heard Matt.

"Hey girls," he said. "What's up?"

"Oh nothing," Mercy answered him. "Just telling the girls how much fun we had tonight."

I had hit the boiling point. Not because of Matt, but because he was being used as a pawn and no one deserved that.

"Hey Mercy! Why don't you tell Matt the truth? You're just using him to get at me, and Alex is the one you really want. I heard everything you said, you lying bitch, and I've had it with your two faces." I emerged from my hiding spot in the bushes. as I spoke and had a moment of satisfaction when I saw the deer-in-the-headlights look in Mercy's expression. But she was smooth and recovered quickly, too quickly for Matt to have seen it as his gaze was focused on me.

At the words, "two faces," I was close enough to drop her with one punch. When she went down, I jumped on top of her and continued punching wherever I could get a shot. Matt tried pulling me off Mercy, but all the yelling had attracted a crowd. Other kids joined in the battle, and Matt was suddenly busy defending himself from some girl and her boyfriend. All of a sudden, the drunk kids from the dance were all around us and a rumble ensued.

Mercy's three girlfriends joined in her defense, and I had four to fight instead of one. I was so mad, and had so much adrenaline coursing through my body, that I just kept at it until I heard the sirens coming our way. Time to bail, I thought. If I got caught it would mean trouble for Ace.

I pulled away from the riot and jumped the fence at the back of the grass field that was adjacent to the ice rink, and ran up and along Bidwell Street until I got to our street. I slowed down then and walked at a regular pace in case the cops happened by.

When I got home, I climbed back through the bedroom window and put on my pajamas. I went to the bathroom to survey the damage. I had a black eye and a few scratches, not too bad. I was just about to head to bed when I heard the doorbell. We had a rule in the West End, no one finks, especially to the cops.

I wondered who it could be when I heard Matt's voice.

"Did Montana make it home okay?"

Damn him! What an idiot! I realized Matt probably knew nothing about my sneaking out. He should've, but he wasn't the sharpest tool in the shed.

"Montana, are you in there?" Danny said as he pounded on the bathroom door.

"Yes," I barely squeaked out.

"Then get your butt out here, girl. You have some explaining to do."

I opened the door. I knew as soon as Danny heard my story he would side with me; he usually did. I wouldn't be surprised if he wanted to find Mercy and slap her around himself.

"Well Montana," Matt said. "I hope you're proud of yourself. Mercy is at the hospital right now getting stitches in a dozen different places."

"So," I said in a frosty manner, "shouldn't you be with her helping her lick her wounds?"

We reverted to our old pattern, and started yelling at each other until Danny yelled louder and told us to shut up.

"Okay, Montana, I want you to tell me everything. Right from the moment you obviously snuck out of the house until you snuck back in."

So, I did. I started with Mercy at the dance and what she had been up to. What I had heard outside of the community centre, everything. When I was done, I looked at Matt and said I was sorry and told him Mercy was just using him. Danny didn't say a word, but his jaw was twitching—the only sign he ever gave that he was angry.

"Montana," Matt said. "You are so full of yourself, and Mercy said that's exactly what you would say. She says you're jealous of her, and from what I've seen, she's right. She is my girlfriend now, so if you so much as lay one finger on her in future, I'll tie you up and drag you home!"

How dare he? Here I am trying to help the dumb oaf, and he attacks my character and then has the nerve to threaten me in my own home.

"I hate you," I screamed as I slapped him. "And if you ever lay so much as one finger on me, Matt, it will be the last bloody thing you do on this earth, understand? You won't walk away."

"You should really stop drinking, Montana, you can't handle your liquor."

He stomped down the stairs. I glanced at Danny. He looked as if his eyes were going to pop out of his head. I had omitted the alcohol in the retelling, and he was furious. I looked to Eddy for support.

"Eddy, you believe me, don't you?"

"Montana, it doesn't matter if I believe you or not. You shouldn't have interfered, and now your ruse is up." Eddy said good night to Dan and left.

"Danny," I said when we were left alone. "Adam knows about Mercy. Ask him."

"Montana, I'm sick of all this crap!" The words exploded out of him as he stamped away from the front door. My calm, cool, brother was seriously losing his shit, and for what, because of what idiot Matt said?

"This is just another example of you dragging everyone into one of your dramas. I'm not talking to Adam or anyone else. What I am going to do is wallop you, and you're going to take it. If Mercy had told the cops, they would have picked you up and taken you down to juvenile detention!" He shouted those last two words. Yanking me by the arm he drew me over to the couch. "Then Ace would have been contacted, and he would have no choice but to call Dad on the rigs. Sometimes, you are so blind you can't see how selfish and impulsive you can be."

Well, I don't think I have to go into detail about what happened next. Let's just say that Danny did what he said he would do and the sting on my backside was no worse than I deserved. I said I was sorry and promised to never sneak out of the window again. *Yeah, right.*

The next morning, Danny put an alarm on my bedroom window to ensure I kept my promise. And later that day, when Ace came home, he was in such a good mood that when he saw my face, he only chuckled and asked me who won.

Danny only shook his head in disgust but was reluctant to ruin Ace's good mood, so chose to say nothing about the previous night, thank God.

Chapter 10

November 1981

That night was a turning point for me, but not in the way you'd expect. It would be the first time the four of us were to be divided, and marked the beginning of a downward spiral for me.

Winter 1980

The next morning there was a letter in our mailbox for Danny. He had been invited to train with some famous artists in New York and Paris for a semester on full scholarship. He was so excited he could hardly contain himself. We decided to splurge by celebrating that evening and went out to Stuart Anderson's Steakhouse for dinner.

Danny expressed his concern about leaving Ace, alone without backup, with him having to shoulder all the responsibility for Alex and me on his own. Alex and I rolled our eyes at each other, but assured him it would all be good.

Danny gave me a look that said he didn't believe me, for a moment, so I did my best to deflect and convince him of all the positives for him being able to have such a unique experience and eventually, he backed off.

Then, when we arrived home, there was a message on the answering machine from Dad. He was coming home for a visit. This was awesome, because he would be with us for Christmas and could spend time with Danny before he left.

We were all excited and got busy in preparation for Dad's return. Ace did some minor repairs that he had been putting off. Alex cleaned the garage.

I did all the laundry and tidying, and Danny painted the kitchen, as it had been looking pretty chewed up. He sanded the cupboards and re-stained them, as well as adding a fresh coat of paint on the walls.

Then he added an artistic flair and painted a floor-to-ceiling mural on one wall in the kitchen of the four of us. Danny's paintings were generally more abstract. He didn't usually do portraits and I think all of us were surprised by how well it turned out.

I'd like to say that everything was hunky-dory from that time on, but things just seemed to get worse. After the fight, Mercy and I were all-out enemies and the rumours were flying around the school. Some were true, most were not, and the girls that Mercy had confided in that night joined her in tormenting me. I don't think a day went by when I didn't turn a street corner somewhere and three or more of them would be there, threatening me with knives or chains.

If my gang of friends was with me, they said and did nothing, just glared at me as they passed. If it was just Chrissie and me, as it often was, I would get her to leave, as I didn't want her involved. I had taken the events of the Halloween fiasco to heart. Danny and Eddy hadn't stood up for me with Matt. That had not only scared me, but left me feeling alone. I made the choice to handle everything on my own from then on. Every run-in with my newly acquired enemies left me feeling resentful toward Danny and Eddy. Had they backed me and told Matt to screw himself, the attacks would never have happened. But it did show me one thing, that I'd become too dependent on their protection and it was time to handle my crap on my own.

There was one exception to my new self-imposed rule, and that was my twin. Alex was the only one I continued to share openly with and only because Chrissie had filled him in even after I'd asked her not to. I don't like sharing what doesn't work in my life, and find it embarrassing. It was a sign of weakness and one I avoided at all costs.

Still, it was a comfort to know that Chrissie and Alex had my back and were there for emotional support if I needed it. A week after the fight, the word spread that Mercy had dumped Matt and was now going out with a well known street dealer named Nick. Matt started dating some girl from Eric Hamber named Amber. It didn't take long for us all to refer to her as *Amber from Hamber*. Ha! too funny! They seemed a good match, so I silently wished them the best. I could be altruistic when I wanted.

There were more changes to our inner circle when Otter started dating another girlfriend of ours, Kim. With Alex having Chrissie, the four of them did a lot of double dating. I was often invited to tag along and sometimes I did, but all their smoochiness was a big turn off.

The days flew by. Alex, Otter, Ralph and I were in the garage going over some new songs when we heard shouts coming from inside the house. A moment later the door opened and there stood dad with a huge grin on his face.

"What does a guy have to do to get some attention around here?"

"Dad!" We yelled as we tripped over one another to get to him first. He opened his arms and pulled us in for a bear hug. "I missed these faces," he pulled back, his eyes roaming over my brother and me.

"Darn, son, we're eye to eye, you're growing too fast." A faint blush stained Alex's cheeks at Dad's words. "And, who is this pretty princess and what have you done with my tomboy daughter?"

I couldn't hold back the giggle. I had taken to spending a little more effort on my wardrobe choices lately instead of pulling on the closest pair of jeans and a t-shirt.

"Montana is trying to get someone's attention, " Alex joked. I shot him a warning look and changed the subject. "He's not the only one who's grown, Dad, look at Ralph and Otter."

Dad turned his focus to the guys and talked with them for a bit. Of course he knew their parents and Ralph's older brother. We'd all been friends since forever. Otter's dad had died a long time ago and it was just him and his mom. Dad asked about her and how she was doing before turning his attention back to Alex and me.

"When are your brothers home?"

"Danny should be here soon and Ace gets home in another hour or two," Alex answered.

"Perfect! That gives me time to hear you boys play." Alex returned to his spot and picked up his guitar. They started with a newer song Dad wouldn't have heard, but they knew well. I stood with Dad, his arm wrapped around me.

Danny found us there a bit later and stood on Dad's other side, while we watched the guys. Alex would be a star one day, I just knew it. He moved like a cat and had all the rockstar moves down pat, but not in a way that mimicked, but ingrained like this was who he was.

A few songs later they called a halt for the day and were wrapping up as Ace came home. We ordered pizza that night and sat in the living room shooting the shit while we ate. Neither Ace nor Danny mentioned the trouble I had been in on Halloween, thankfully. If the character changes I'd gone through since then were evident, no one commented, but I was very aware I was quieter, more like Alex. It wasn't real, just a result of going through shit I chose not to share. The truth was, I was dying inside.

Two days after Christmas, we drove Danny out to the airport to say goodbye and send him off to New York. Some of his art buddies were there to wish him bon voyage, including Adam. As I watched Danny walk through the gate, I suddenly felt very lonely. Our foursome had never been split, and I felt like part of me was leaving.

"Danny, wait!" I called as I ran down the ramp toward him.

"Hey, little sis, what's up?"

"I'm sorry I was such a monster before and I need to know before you get on that plane that you forgive me. Please, Danny, tell me you forgive me. I'm going to miss you so much," I said, as the tears tracked down my cheeks.

"Hey, no tears, and of course I forgive you, silly. I love you."

I felt better and let him go with promises that he would write to me often. Later that night, I overheard Dad and Ace talking in the living room.

"Is everything okay, son? I mean, are you handling everything okay? I know taking care of a household and going to school, as well as working part-time, is a lot on your plate. Really, it's unfair all the responsibility you have. You know if something went wrong, I would be home in a heartbeat, right?"

Ace assured him that everything was cool and he was handling everything fine. Ace also mentioned that I wanted to take dance classes and had already picked out the school I wished to attend. Dad said I could as long as my grades didn't slack. He never had to say that stuff about Alex who was a straight-A student and never had to study, whereas I struggled just to keep up a B average.

Alex got Ace's brain, who in turn got the brains from my mom. They were naturally intelligent, gifted students, a teacher's dream. In every other way Alex resembled Danny: artistic, funny, easy going, and philosophic. "It is what it is," he was fond of saying. Neither Danny nor Alex ever burnt out; they always worked at an appropriate energy level. Whereas, Ace and I were similar in that we burnt out frequently; we tended to be more like that little Eveready bunny on the commercials. We got that from our dad.

A few days later Dad left and the house got quiet. It didn't take long for a pit of dread to start growing in my stomach. When I keeled over after lunch at school one day, Ace took me to the doctor where we discovered that I had an ulcer.

When I was being diagnosed, the doctor asked questions about my life. Like, if I liked school and those types of things. I told him nothing of my growing depression or of the relentless torment by the girls at school. The doc talked to Ace privately, who in turn questioned me on the way home. I was evasive and told him nothing of my thoughts or feelings.

It was in the new dance classes I started after Dad left that I began to feel better. I could go into the studio in any mood and by the time class was over I'd be feeling free and happy. My body was becoming my art and I shared many things I was learning with the cheerleading squad.

Our performances at the games got better as we became a tighter, more unified team. I loved being head cheerleader. I loved the girls and the performance and kept my focus on dance and the squad.

We got a call from Dad one day, saying he was working close to New York and he and Danny were spending a few days together, just the two of them. I imagined my brother's excitement with having Dad to himself, and heard all about their fun in the letters he sent home.

Danny had promised me he'd write to me weekly and he kept that promise. His letters were a highlight and overflowed with enthusiasm and excitement. I did my best to keep him informed of all that was happening on our end. By comparison, my letters to him were a lot less enthusiastic but if he noticed, he never said anything in his letters to me about it.

Ace was around very little as he was dividing his time and giving what was left to Kristine. Alex and I saw him on Sunday nights for dinner, and he was there to help with homework afterward. Ace only brought Kristine over a few times. She would go out to the garage to hear Alex and the band rehearse. I didn't spend any effort in getting to know her. To me, she was the girl who took my brother away. Selfish attitude, I know, but those were my feelings.

I might have made the effort if he'd included us in his happiness a bit more, but he mostly kept them separate from his family. I spent the bulk of my weekends in the company of Eddy and Pat, who would come down on the weekends from Abbotsford and stay in the spare room at Eddy's.

The advantage to hanging with those guys was I could drink and not have to disguise it. I could trust them, heck, everybody trusted them! The thought entered my head a few times that this could be bad for my body, but in truth, I didn't drink that much if it was just the three of us and no one seemed to care anyway. My attitude was if no one cared then why should I? In fact, it was this very attitude that got me into my next situation.

Chapter 11

November 1981

The picture cards shifted to Danny's letters, photos and poems he sent on his first trip away from home. How I had missed him and had wanted to tell him everything going on in my life. My support of his opportunity was a way of showing him that I was perfectly capable of standing on my own two feet. And... It was my way of sticking it to the man, so to speak. If everything went sideways, and it did, I knew I could blame him for everything.

If Danny hadn't left, he would have made sure everything was working. That was his job, to balance the scales in the house. Ace was too extreme in one direction, and me in the other, Danny was the middleman who made it all work.

Selfish! That single word filtered out all else. I got it, all I could think of was me, and my misfortunes, and then blame Danny. When in reality, I chose not to communicate, not to ask for help, not to share how I felt. If I had, perhaps what happened next might not have happened.

January 1981

Chrissie and I had gone downtown for a girls' shopping trip. She had a date that night with my brother, Otter and Kim, and was excited to show off her new threads. We parted ways at the school and I headed home. Alex was just heading out when I arrived. I had left her at the school, as she was going home to drop off her bags and get changed for her date with Alex. When I arrived home, Alex was just about to walk out the door to head over to Chrissie's.

"He, Eddy just called and said Pat has just arrived and they're waiting for you to come over. I thought you were coming to the movies with us?"

He seemed kinda put out that I'd made alternate plans. I didn't tell him that watching him and my best friend make out in the theatre grossed me out, so I just said I wasn't up to a movie. Alex grabbed his keys and stopped long enough to give me a penetrating look.

"When are you going to stop acting like a lost lamb, Montana? It's getting really boring. You've been a self-absorbed jerk since Danny left. We all miss him. You're not the only one. Move on with your life, little girl. I'm going. Are you coming with me?"

"No, but thanks for that inspiring speech, brother, and I'm not a little girl, if that were true then you'd be a little boy. We're twins, remember!" Just saying that made me sound like I was ten years old.

He just smirked like I'd just proved his point and slammed the door on his way out. I phoned Eddy back to say I couldn't join them. I said I had homework to do. Truth is I needed some alone time. A date with myself and a mickey of rum and the 7-11.

Blake and Blair Carrington were standing outside when I arrived. The twins were new to the school this year and both were excellent basketball players. I knew them from practices and games although we'd not spent time together outside of the court.

"Hey, Montana," they said in unison. "What are you up to?"

In response, I opened up my bomber jacket so they could see the mickey of rum in my jacket.

Their eyes took in my full bottle greedily. "Feel like sharing?" they asked in unison.

"No probs, guys. Let's get our Cokes and we'll meet back outside."

When we were done, and back outside, we poured out half our Cokes and filled it with rum. "Keep it real," I said as I turned to leave.

"Hey, Montana, we're going to a party," Blake said. "Do you want to join us?" Blair added. I didn't have to think about it, and accepted the invitation. Maybe a party was just what I needed to blow off some steam and take my mind off things.

The Carrington brothers didn't know me well, which made them perfect companions for the evening. I wouldn't have had to avert my eyes with them like I would have at the theatre, or be under the microscope like I had been with

Eddy and Pat of late. Besides, what could be more natural, than the star basketball players and the head cheerleader going to a party?

The place was packed when we got there. A grade eleven girl I didn't know was having the party. She held it in a huge rec room. It had a wet bar, a pool table and two pinball machines.

A shit ton of people roamed around the basement and outside where they were allowed to smoke whatever they'd brought with them, not my scene at all. We grabbed beers from behind the bar and made our way over to the pool table. We received lots of looks but as I said, before, cheerleader and basketball players was not such a stretch, despite this being our first time in public together.

Pat and Eddy arrived when we were finishing our game. and both looked a little pissed off with me..

"Look guys. I had every intention of studying, but I wanted a walk first and ran into the brothers. No harm, no foul, just chill."

Eddy accepted what I said, but when he and Pat moved over to the bar, they sat down on a couple of stools and kept their eyes on me. It was hard not to stick out my tongue. God! I could be so juvenile. I really needed to learn how to express myself one day, but for tonight I was content to turn around and roll my eyes.

Blake chuckled. "So, what is the deal with you and Eddy?" he asked. "I thought you two were going out because you're always together." Blair added.

"He's been my neighbor since before I was born. He's one of my closest friends, and totally cool." They nodded their heads like that explained everything when in reality it didn't even come close to who Eddy was to me. How many times had he been there for me? Too damn many to count.

"Hey, Mo, doesn't one of your brothers, the one with the football scholarship, work at London Drugs?"

"Yeah, that's Ace," I replied.

"I've seen him play," Blake said. "He's a powerhouse! I heard just the other day that he's getting married."

I almost dropped my beer can on the shag rug. "What the hell are you talking about Blake, and where did you hear that?"

"Blair's best friend works at London Drugs; he talks to Ace when they're on the same shift. He told me Ace said he might drop the rest of his scholarship so he can get married."

I couldn't believe I didn't see this coming. Of course, Ace would consider marriage. He was at the age, and he was smitten with Kristine. I felt sick to my stomach. How could he not have told us? "Yeah, yeah, I don't know how serious he is though, it's still just talk at this point." I had to say something and that's what came out of my mouth despite the fact that I was almost dizzy with shock. "Let's get some shooters," I added and grabbing both their hands, steered them back to the bar.

We pounded back four each and were grabbing some more beer when Mercy showed up with her new boyfriend Nick. I watched him work the room and had to admit there was something appealing about him. If it wasn't for his drug dealing and the fact he'd quit school, I might have befriended him.

What was I thinking? He was with Mercy, I would never befriend him.

Blake knew Nick and invited the two of them to join us in a game of pool. Blake must have been the only guy in school who was unaware of the animosity between Mercy and me. Halfway through our game, Matt and Amber-from-Hamber arrived. Amber joined a few girls she had met, and Matt joined Eddy and Pat at the bar. I observed the three of them watching me. I acted oblivious to their staring, but I was pretty sure Eddy was keeping tabs on the amount of alcohol I was consuming. If I didn't watch my actions, he might haul my butt out of there.

Blake and I finished our beer at the same time, so while he was racking and talking to Nick, I sauntered up to the bar to get more. "I have one question for you guys," I slurred my words. "Did you know about Ace getting married?"

Matt looked surprised, but Pat and Eddy, although saying nothing, didn't bat an eye at the question. Figures, I thought, two of my best buddies ever, and they knew about Ace and didn't tell me. I grabbed the beer, while shooting a look of disgust at Eddy, and followed Blake and Nick outside to smoke up before our game.

Mercy was already there but that suited me fine. I could handle her as long as she didn't say anything. A moment later, Matt came outside and joined our little pot smoking group.

"Let's hope Montana can hold her pot as well as her liquor," Mercy said. "We wouldn't want a repeat of last time, now, would we?" she finished with a smirk.

"Shut up, Mercy. Your little posse isn't here to protect you this time. I don't think Matt here is up for saving your pathetic ass after the way you treated him last time."

Everyone was quiet as they sensed the hate in the air and the fight about to take place.

"Hey Montana, why don't you lighten up? We're just here for some laughs, okay?" The first words Nick had ever spoken to me, and Mercy looked pissed off that he hadn't said something threatening instead. If I had been in my right mind, I probably would have taken what he said and laughed and said okay. I wasn't in my right mind, however, and hadn't been for a while.

"Hey, Nick, I hope you know she's using you the same way she uses everyone else. As soon as she gets bored or she no longer gets what she needs, she'll spit you out just like she did to Matt. So, you and your "girlfriend" can go screw yourselves!"

I walked away after that statement and headed for home. Blake came running after me to make sure I was okay. I assured him I was and sent him back to the party. A few minutes later, Matt and Amber came by in his car and offered me a ride, but I turned that down too.

I was drunk, stoned and feeling betrayed by my family and friends. I alternated between laughing and crying as I wove my way home. I was about two blocks away when I saw a black Nova trailing me. I was too tired and messed up to care. I fell on the grass and threw up. When I was done, I sat and waited for them to make their move.

The car pulled over. Mercy, Nick and some others got out of the car. They had followed me for a reason and I'm sure it wasn't to offer me a ride. I staggered to my feet and said in my coolest voice, "Did you miss me?"

No one spoke as they made a ring around me and closed in and I recognized it for what it was, a shake down. "If you're looking for a fight, you got one." I fought hard, but was pretty intoxicated and had little steam. It didn't take long for two of them to pin me down while the others worked me over. The last thing I remember before I passed out was a voice saying, "There she is."

I woke up in a bright, white place, and for a second, I thought I was dead and in heaven. "Where am I?" I whispered in a low, groggy voice.

"In the hospital," a voice answered.

I found out later that I had been in and out of consciousness for three days. On the third, I awoke and saw a lump on a chair beside my bed. The lump was Ace.

My brother must have felt me looking at him, because he opened his eyes and gave me a grin when he saw me awake.

"What happened?" I muttered.

Ace yawned and scrubbed his face before replying. "You were jumped a few days ago by a gang. They worked you over pretty good. You have three broken ribs, three more that are cracked, and stitches in a few places, and a mild concussion. Eddy and Pat found you and brought you to the hospital. I'm surprised Eddy isn't here right now. He hasn't left the hospital since he brought you in."

The party... something I heard about Ace. "I was attacked by some kids who were at the same party as me. The one where I found out you're engaged, you traitor." Ace looked surprised but didn't deny it.

"Montana, I haven't called Dad or Danny, yet. I didn't know what to tell them about what happened to you."

He totally just ignored what I'd said and turned the focus back on me. Alex walked through the door. "It's about time you woke up, slacker," he pulled over a chair on the opposite side from Ace and sat with one foot crossed over his knee. "How you feeling?"

"Like I've been hit by a truck, but that's not the worst part."

"Oh?" His eyes narrowed. "What's the worst part?"

"I guess you weren't in the know either."

"Montana, I'm very confused right now, is this the concussion talking?"

"Our brother is getting married." Alex's eyes grew wide, but he made no comment. When Ace left the room without any explanation, Alex and I speculated about how our lives would change with Ace married.

The next day I got to go home with strict instructions to stay in bed. No argument from me, as the ribs hurt big time. When we arrived home, Alex bustled around the kitchen making us tea and talking a mile a minute. Alex and I loved tea. When we were little and our older brothers were at school, Mom made us tea and we had parties.

Alex served it up in the same little porcelain cups that Mom used to use. Holding it brought back those feelings of being loved and cherished. Inevitably, feelings of loss followed. Maybe it was because of the painkillers, or maybe because I'd been shut off for quite a while. I don't know what it was, but suddenly I was overcome and what started as a few tears tracking down my cheeks quickly turned into a steady stream. A sob escaped, morphing into heavy crying, and I clutched my ribs, a combination of being upset and the pain. My twin tried to comfort me but he was also feeling all my stuff.

The medical profession has done studies proving that twins can feel each other's turmoil: sadness, pain, and happiness, etc. Alex choked out that he knew when I was getting beat up and he had looked for me but couldn't find me. We embraced and… well, that's how Ace found us a few minutes later… hugging and crying like a couple of babies.

"What are you two getting on about?" he asked. "What's going on? What's wrong?"

"We miss Mom," I cried.

"And Dad and Danny," Alex added, "and now you're leaving us, too," we said at the same time.

Ace sighed and sat down opposite us in dad's chair—Ace's chair when dad wasn't there. "Look, I don't know who has been telling you what, but I have to set the record straight. I have some things to say to you both. What you heard is partially true. I did talk to my boss, and I did ask him if he would hire me full time as a manager. The thing is,

Kristine thought she was pregnant, and I wanted to do the right thing. I'm in love with her."

Our eyes got as big as saucers, but we said nothing and let Ace continue.

"I have two years left of university, Kristine has four, and the last thing we want at this point is a baby. I already have a family to support, a family that needs me." He said this last part looking directly at me.

"Like I said, I was prepared to do the right thing. Then Mo, while you were in the hospital, we found out it was a false alarm. The night you got beat up, I wasn't here because Kristine and I were out celebrating. I'm not leaving you guys and neither is Dan. I'm really sorry I didn't tell you earlier, but I know you have both been preoccupied, and I didn't want to burden you with my stuff."

I was shocked by what he'd shared and for the first time saw that Ace was not just my brother and guardian, he was also a guy, a twenty-one-year old man who was trying to have something for himself.

"When I got home," Ace continued, "Pat was here waiting for me, to fill me in on what had happened. I raced over to the hospital, and when I saw you, Mo, I felt ashamed of myself for not seeing where you were at. I want you to know I'm sorry, and I will pay better attention to your needs."

"I'm the one who's sorry, Ace," I replied. "I didn't keep my end of the bargain. It's just easier to blame you for everything. I was tired of getting dissed because of 'stuff' happening. Thought I would try quiet stoicism for a bit... turns out, that doesn't work for me," I said with a grin.

"*Hmmmp*," was all he said. But his worry lines smoothed out a bit as he said, "Okay, Montana, your turn to spill. I have an itchy fist and I want to know everything. Alex, go and make some more tea."

While Alex went to make more tea, I told Ace how I had been feeling. I told him about everything from the Halloween dance to the present, omitting nothing this time. I told him about Danny spanking me, the alcohol, everything.

When Alex entered the room with the tea, I continued my retelling. I let Alex know that I had been feeling left out of his life, and although I loved him and Chrissie, being with them while they were all lovey-dovey bugged me. I finished up my narration by revealing my indulgence of pot at the party, the conversation outside, and who followed me home. I could see Ace processing and weighing out his course of action. Whatever it was going to be, I thought with a yawn, I sure didn't want to be any of those guys. Ace said that was enough for one night, and I promptly lay back and fell asleep.

The next evening Adam and Kristine dropped by. Adam had a package that Dan had sent to him to be delivered to me and Kristine came to help Ace make dinner. As getting up and sitting up was incredibly painful, the group sat with me in the living room while we ate dinner and chatted about nothing in particular.

Kristine caught a moment alone with me after dinner when she took my plate from me, and while Adam graced the rest of the group with amusing stories keeping the mood light and fun, Kristine apologized for everything that had happened and said that she wanted to be friends.

"No problems, Kristine, we can be friends as long as you take me out shopping in that cool car of yours when I'm better."

She laughed. "Nothing would please me more than getting to spend some quality time with the one person who keeps Ace on his toes. She winked and I grinned. Kristine had potential as my future sister-in-law as long as it was way, way in the future.

Eddy came by after dinner, and he and Ace disappeared into Ace's room for a while. When they resurfaced, Eddy came over to talk to me.

"Montana, I want you to know that Mercy, Nick, and her posse won't be bothering you anymore, I've taken care of it." He could tell I wanted to ask a million questions, but held up his hand in a stop fashion.

"We're not going to discuss it. It has been taken care of. You put up with it for way too long and beyond the point of being able to deal with it on your own—I think we need colours. Yellow could be a colour for when things are starting to get tough, red could be the colour for your call for help."

"Huh?"

"Well, you see, everyone has soft edges and hard edges, and everyone's edges are as different as their personalities. What may be a hard edge to you, may be a soft one to me, and vice versa."

I must have looked confused because he continued.

"Okay, it's like this. Say you don't like to be touched, it's a soft edge, and when someone passes you in the hallway at school, and their shoulder accidentally grazes yours, you notice, but as it is not a direct touch, you're okay with it. Then say someone passes you in the hall and they purposely elbow you. You become furious or upset because they've crossed a hard edge or boundary with you." I nodded my head in understanding.

"If you can begin to look at what you consider to be your hard edges, then you will begin to understand when you should ask for help. Because hard edges include what happens 'to you' when people don't respect you, meaning being bullied and beaten up. Those are hard edges for most, if not all, people. That's when you should seek our help, mine and your brothers."

"But, Eddy," I began, "you told me I needed to start handling my stuff on my own and to stop getting everyone else to bail me out when I get in over my head."

"You're right," he replied. "I did say that, but I was referring to situations you get into that you know better than to get into. You need to learn to quit while you're ahead instead of burying yourself deeper. You would never have learned it if we always kept bailing you out, *capeesh*?" He did his best Italian mafia voice with that last word and it was hard not to giggle, but doing so would have hurt like hell.

"Yeah, Eddy, I got it. Maybe I'm not as tough as I would like you all to believe."

He grinned and kissed my cheek, probably the only piece of me that didn't hurt.

It was almost time for me to get back to sleep, and I still hadn't seen the present that Adam had brought over.

Everyone sat down, and Adam handed me the gift while he read the letter out loud for everyone to hear.

"Dearest Montana,

I'm sure you don't mind Adam fulfilling this request for me as I am away and you seem to have a soft spot for him."

My cheeks went bright crimson and the rest laughed while Adam continued.

"I know you are finding your way in the world, and sometimes it isn't easy. Sometimes we can forget who we are and where we came from. Get Ace to tell you about that time Dad tanned his ass real good and you'll realize you're not the only brat in the family."

It was Ace's turn to blush, and Kristine elbowed him in the ribs while Adam read on.

"The painting that Adam has brought is a tribute to who you are and how I see you, how I've always seen you, beautiful and full of vitality.

One last thing, I will be home a bit early, so I will be there for your and Alex's birthday.

I love you and miss you,

Danny xo"

I was so touched by his letter and it couldn't have come at a better time. I tore the paper off the frame as Adam held it. Many sharp inhalations were drawn when the painting was revealed. No one commented, just took in its beauty. The painting was a water colour of me in my cheerleading gear leaping in the air. The way he did it, I appeared to leap right off the page.

It was incredible, and as everyone gathered and found their tongues, many comments were made. New York had done amazing things to grow his talent. He was always good, but the painting was indicative—my new grown up word—of his growth.

What a wonderful gift, a wonderful evening, and a turnaround from the last few months. Despite my pain, I felt happier than I had in a really long time. I hobbled to the kitchen and looked at the mural on the kitchen wall. I leaned forward and gave the image of Dan a kiss.

"Thanks, Dan the Man, you're the best," I said, and made my way back to the living room.

Chapter 12

November 1981

Mmm, that evening was a turning point. Slowly things began to get better, at least for a while.

March 1981

Time flew and the countdown was on for Danny's return. Alex and I brainstormed ways we could make him feel welcomed home. After hours of lame suggestions, Chrissie came up with an idea to do an overhaul on his room. The three of us entered his room to see what type of condition it was in.

Months of dust and no air had taken a toll, and it hadn't been exactly tidy when he'd left. We opened his window to air it out, dusted, vacuumed, organized, and washed his bedding. After remaking his bed, we completed our effort by placing a fresh vase of daisies on his night stand.

The next day was difficult. I could barely focus on anything but seeing Danny, and seeing my brother wasn't the only caveat for me. As Ace had school, Adam would be waiting outside after our last class to take us with him to the airport.

When the bell finally rang, it was a race down the stairs between the two of us. I arrived a split second ahead of my brother and got to ride shotgun. Alex didn't seem to mind though, shooting me a raised eyebrow and a smirk when Adam did up my seat belt and closed my door. I blushed but kept my mouth shut. Adam got in the driver's seat and off we went.

I was so excited I couldn't stop squirming.

"Montana," Adam said, "this reminds me of the first time I met you."

"Oh really, Adam, and why is that?" I asked.

"You were so fidgety that night, I figured you hated being in my company. Now I know you were just excited about being in my company."

Alex and Adam had a great chuckle at my expense. I averted my gaze as the heat spread quickly from my chest to my cheeks. Why was I constantly blushing around this man? Never before had anyone had an affect on me the way Adam did. He made me feel sexy and naughty at the same time and we'd never even kissed.

The night Adam brought the painting over, he'd given me a large, well worn Webster Dictionary, and challenged me to learn two new words a day. It was meant to occupy my mind while I was healing, but it felt like more than that, like somehow this was a test. I scanned through the new and interesting words I'd learned to describe how Adam made me feel... discombobulated! Ha! Thank you Webster's Dictionary.

The plane arrived and Danny was the first one off. He looked really good; I'd forgotten how drop-dead gorgeous he was. Danny and Adam shared otherworldly good looks, like Greek gods, that's how gorgeous they were. The two of them looked more related to each other than Danny did to our brothers.

Alex and I were jumping up and down, waving and I'm sure looking idiotic in our enthusiasm. As Danny came closer, I studied his appearance. He'd matured and looked older. He was glowing with vitality which only added more appeal to his already good looks. He wore clothes I hadn't seen before which meant he'd shopped in New York. Everyone knew they were easily ahead of us by three years in the fashion department and my brother's new threads were testimony of that. He looked like money. I glanced around and noticed women of all ages watching him as he strutted toward us.

The work Danny had done abroad had already been shipped home. Alex and I wanted to open it, but Ace said that was like reading someone else's mail. Alex and I had no problem opening someone else's mail, but in the end Ace won. We left the art in the living room still wrapped.

My thoughts broke when Danny flung himself at me and Alex for hugs.

"I missed you guys so much! Alex, you got taller and, Mo, you look older."

"Well, she was busy while you were gone," Adam said with a wink.

"Hey buddy," Danny said, giving Adam a hug. "Thanks for picking me up and bringing the kids with you." He was laughing when he said that last part. The joke was on him... Alex had grown and was taller than both of them. With his casual grunge look and quiet intelligence, he could have been mistaken as the older sibling. How had I not noticed before now?

Adam and Danny sat in the front seat chatting about art-related topics that went right over my head. Instead of inserting myself and sounding like an idiot, I sat back and enjoyed listening to the flow of their chat. With my brother back in Canada, my life felt complete, like his absence had created an empty space that daily living hadn't been able to fill.

Ace was home when we arrived, and in a flash, he was down the porch steps and picking up Danny like he weighed no more than a child, and swung him around like a rag doll. He gave him a back breaking bear hug and didn't let go until Danny complained of not being able to breathe. Adam said he wanted to give us our family "bonding" time and was leaving.

I walked him to his car to thank him once more for taking us with him. There was a whole lot more I wanted to say but I kept my mouth shut. He winked before driving off, leaving my heart in a fluttering mess. "One day," I sighed. "Yeah, but today isn't that day." I turned off anymore thinking about Adam and quickly returned to the house.

That night we had a homecoming feast. We sat at the table for hours eating great food and listening to story after story of Danny's adventures. Many I had heard already from his letters, and many that were new. We had stories to tell also. The best one Alex told. Otter got caught shoplifting and the judge had given him community time. Yep, Otter was the newest addition to the ostrich pen at the Vancouver Aquarium! Every weekend Otter spent half a day cleaning and tending to the ostrich's needs.

The story went that one ostrich in particular fell hard for Otter and would chase him around the pen. Otter would have to use a hose to keep the ostrich at bay while he was inside. Another kid who received the same sentence as Otter would work with him. One day the kid, while on the outside of the pen, turned the water valve off. So, when Otter went to turn the hose on to keep the ostrich away, nothing came out. Otter dropped the hose and was over the ten-foot fence in about ten seconds.

"As for the ostrich... the poor thing is in therapy for depression," Alex finished. We were howling with laughter at Otter's expense.

With dinner finished, it was time to present Danny with his surprise. We blindfolded him and walked to his room, and as Alex took the blindfold off, I turned on the light. Danny's eyes lit up.

"You guys are the best! I figured I would be sleeping on the couch tonight."

"Well, judging by the amount of art that arrived today, I don't think there is any room for you there." Alex smirked.

Danny chuckled. "It's all so surreal, being back and everything is the same, but I'm not the same."

I wanted to ask him what he'd meant by that but he was tired from the time change and travel and said goodnight.

Danny spent the next week hanging with us and his friends, just relaxing and catching up before his school got underway again. During that time, we decided to get a group of us together and take in a movie at the drive-in theatre in Surrey by the Patullo Bridge. Three carloads headed there to see Raiders of the Lost Ark. Pat and some of his buddies came down from Abbotsford and met up with us.

When it was over, we headed for home. The second feature didn't look that good, and we were restless, so we decided a jam session in the garage was in order. The guys had some new songs they wanted to play for us. Of course, I knew the songs, as I had written most of them.

I didn't write a single word during my depression, but now, with my world right-side up again, I was like a bubbling spring, bursting with ideas and words. There was a lot to say, so much that if the guys ever got a recording contract, they had enough songs to fill up a few albums. Writing for them was the easiest way for me to express myself without having to have conversations.

The next song was one of my newest, and def my favorite from the new batch. A slow lyrical song that described tough times.

It IsWhat It Is.

"It is what it is so they say
my drink's gone flat and lost its taste

in the usual way something inside is going wrong
I know I've gotta be strong I don't know what's missing
friends in love
make me sick with their kissing
I just need to be alone
it is what it is
as I look at the phone when are you going to be home
now I've got a pain so deep inside nobody sees it I've gotta hide
where is the salve for the wound in my soul
all I want is to go for a ride
but the pain in my ribs is real
no one can see what I feel
It is what it is that's just the way that it is
It is what it is
and there's nothing I can do.

I wanted to keep my eyes on the floor and not see what they were feeling. But like a car accident, I had to see the reaction like blood and death and all those things that hold our attention. The pain reflected in every face held me captive, until I broke the spell by leaving the room.

I felt like my world had collided, by hearing aloud, all my inner demons, with no external filter to water it down. What had been roiling inside of me was powerful and sad. It rang of aloofness and segregation.

When I came back in the garage, the guys were playing a happy, upbeat song, one Alex had written.

Eddy smiled at me and winked from across the room. Danny came and stood by my side with his arm around me;

thankfully, no one said a word, or I would have lost my shit and falling apart with witnesses was so not cool.

Chapter 13

November 1981

Danny's return marked a new chapter. In some ways things returned to normal and the angst I'd experienced in the time he was away was no longer an issue for me. I'd shifted my perspective somewhat, seeing both my elder brothers as more than just family, but as men who would one day have lives of their own. I didn't like to think about that a whole lot. I wasn't ready for that type of upheaval. Time would prove that I wasn't ready for a lot of what happened.

April 1981

Basketball season was in full swing, after Danny's homecoming, and my life was all about cheerleading. The girls and I came up with some new cheers and found ourselves getting geared up as much as the guys for the playoffs.

We were the Dragons, and we were very patriotic about our school and team. One of the coolest things about the students at our school is that we were committed to its success and our own, despite its below average size.

Located in the heart of the west end of Vancouver, King George High School housed approximately three hundred students, ranging from grade eight to twelve. There was no segregation in our community of students, as everyone pretty much knew everyone. It wasn't uncommon to see a grade eight student hanging out with a grade twelve student. I believed it was that reason our games were so well attended. The bleachers were always packed, the stage across from them lined up with chairs and the standing room only by the doors also full.

The weekend of our semi playoffs was no different. Friday night the atmosphere was like a party and we kicked ass, guaranteeing us a spot for the finals on Sunday. Saturday four teams competed and we came in second. Everyone left exhausted. We didn't have a full second string so most of the guys had played continually. The cheerleaders had taken it upon ourselves to ensure there were plenty of Snickers bars and Ginger Ale for our team to keep them going.

Sunday was like a homecoming. Being down to two teams, the energy was less aggressive but more intense. Whereas Saturday attendees did a lot of shouting and cheering from the stands. Sunday you could almost hear a pin drop between the bounces of the ball on the court. Many of our old elementary school gang came out to support us and it was nice seeing so many familiar faces that we didn't see often anymore. They had new friends with them and after the game we got to know them. An entire new crew of friends from the west side came with lots of party invites, one for the following Saturday, which the girls and I accepted.

The band was playing in a jazz club on the west side the night of the party so we could help them set up, go to the party, and then come back, and we could all go home together.

Sonya, Leigh and Michelle, our old buddies, met us at Waves, and we bussed from there to the upper West Side and met up with our new buddies: Dave, Ben, Cole, Robert, Clark, Shelley, Judy and Chandra.

It was a nice neighborhood and the party was being held in the basement of a large house. When we entered, there were teens everywhere, leaning against walls and having someone press on their chest, then they'd pass out. What kind of weird crap were they into?

Shelly guided us through the room explaining that they were hyperventilating and when someone pressed on their chest they'd lose consciousness. Apparently this was cool. I thought they were nuts but of course had to try it a few times before deciding it wasn't for me.

In the backyard, teens were crawling around on the lawn picking mushrooms. "Shelley, what are they doing?"

"Duh, picking magic mushrooms." she replied.

"What is a magic mushroom and how is it you have magic mushrooms in your yard?"

Shelley laughed. "You West End girls are kinda naive. The mushrooms are hallucinogenic, like acid."

"Ohhh. I've never done acid."

"None of us have," Chrissie added.

"How many do you have to eat to get going, you know, get high?" I had to know if we decided to try, how many we'd have to eat.

"Well, Montana, weight and sensitivity play a part, but in general, ten will do it. These ones are quite small, so maybe a handful would be good. Come with me, and I'll show you how to pick the right ones."

Chrissie, Kim and I followed Shelley around the yard to learn the art of selection. We crawled and picked and would show them to Shelley before we ate them. Being the brilliant girls we were, we forgot to ask how fast-acting the mushrooms were. It wasn't long before Kim, the tiniest in stature of our group, abruptly sat down and just stared off into space.

"What's up with you, Kim?" I asked.

She didn't answer me. I looked at Shelley for an explanation. Before Shelley could say anything, Kim broke out in laughter, and she just kept on laughing.

"Can't you see it?" she finally choked out. "It's right over there," she said, pointing.

The three of us looked at where she was pointing but saw nothing.

"The dancing pink elephants," she said. "They're so damn funny!"

Oh, she was seriously delusional, and we would soon be joining her. I would have to get us out of here fast, before I was as non-functional as her. No bus, we needed a cab. When it kicked in, Chrissie and I would be just like that, and I didn't know how much time we had as we'd all consumed different amounts and we were all different weights. I was the tallest and by default the heaviest, fingers crossed, I would be functioning longer than the two of them.

"Shelley, call me a cab, and tell them to hurry. I have to meet up with the guys before Chrissie is as messed up as Kim. One I can handle, but two, no way!"

Shelley left to call the cab, and I grabbed Kim and hauled her to her feet. I pushed her up the stairs and out the front door. Then, I literally carried her to the fence at the front of the yard. I went back for Chrissie and found her almost exactly where Kim had been, and she was laughing, but at what, I had no idea. I was starting to feel the effects of the mushrooms and knew I was running out of time.

I picked up Chrissie—thank God, I am tall and athletic—and managed to carry her out to Kim and deposit her on the ground beside her. Thankfully, the cabbie showed up a moment later, and I gave him the address as I sunk back in the seat.

When we arrived at the club, I reached into my pocket to get out the money to pay, and discovered that the veins in my arms were moving like worms. I started to laugh and barely got myself and the other two out of the vehicle.

Luckily, the guys were just exiting the club for a break.

Ralph's older brother was picking the equipment up. He usually did, and we'd unload the next day. We paid him gas money and an extra twenty for helping us out. Tonight, he was early, as he had taken in the show and was talking with the guys. Alex waved and came over to give Chrissie a kiss; as he leaned in, she screamed, and Kim and I burst out laughing.

Chrissie's reaction so surprised Alex, that he jumped about two feet in the air. To me he resembled a giant raven and looked like he was flying.

"Alex, do it again; oh again, please!"

"Do what again, Mo? What's wrong with you all, anyway?"

During all of this, I found out later that Kim and I had been killing ourselves laughing the entire time, but all I remembered was everything appearing to be in black and white and moved like a slow-motion movie.

Alex grabbed my arm and gave me a shake.

"Montana, what the hell is wrong with you guys? Are you drunk?"

When Alex spoke, his voice suddenly switched from slow into fast forward and sounded like Alvin and the Chipmunks. This started a fresh peal of laughter from me.

"Alex," I managed to gasp out. "We, uh, ate a few mushrooms, and well, umm, you're looking pretty damned funny right now."

I could see him pondering what to do and come to a decision. Again, everything is playing out in slow mode. I have never seen with so much clarity before, the lines in his face, the obvious thoughts passing though his features. His eyes.

I saw him like I had never seen him before. I saw Alex past his features, and it was cool.

"Listen, Montana, I'm sending you home in a cab with Eddy, he and Pat are inside and Dillon will help us take down and drive us home. All of you stay there until this wears off and we will be there as soon as we can. Montana, do you understand me? If so, nod your head."

I nodded my head. The next thing I remember was getting out of the cab at our house. I went to use the bathroom. When I stood to flush the toilet, I saw the poster of *Jaws* coming out of the toilet. Danny had put that poster up on the bathroom wall years ago. I started screaming as Jaws broke free of his porcelain prison and leapt to eat me. Eddy came bounding through the bathroom door.

"What the hell is going on in here?" he asked.

"The toilet. Jaws... he's here and he wants to eat me!"

"Montana," Eddy said with a laugh, while guiding me to the living room. "Jaws couldn't fit in the bathroom, never mind the toilet. I hope you girls come down soon. You're all so freaking weird right now."

It wasn't long after the bathroom incident that the mushrooms wore off. I was infused with clarity in a way I'd never experienced before, like those moments earlier with Alex, seeing beneath the everyday. Chrissie and Kim felt the same, and our shared experience brought on a deep philosophical conversation.

I spoke of things that I normally never shared with anyone. I opened up about school and Adam, and shared in ways that I normally never would have. The fun part was the girls did also, and even Eddy, although he resisted at first.

The next day things were back to normal and although the events of the previous night were blurred at best, the residue of having real conversation for probably the first time in my life stayed. I felt a new level of friendship in my relationship with the girls and Eddy. A camaraderie that I fully planned on nurturing.

Chapter 14

November 1981

Eddy and Chrissie would become so much more than just my best friends. The challenges that tested me and my family would require more than just friendship from them, but also complete reliance in some ways, but it wasn't theirs to keep solely, others came in to share that burden and it is to them that I feel the most guilt for being here.

May 1981

"Two days, Mo, just two more days, until we're one year older!" I was grinning from ear to ear at Alex's enthusiasm. I'd never seen him so excited about a birthday before. We didn't know what our brothers had planned as yet, just that something was going to happen.

It was with anticipation that we sat down at our kitchen table for dinner that evening. Ace said he wanted to discuss birthday plans with us, and we couldn't wait to hear what he had up his sleeve. Ace took his time getting around to the topic. When he finally did, it was to inform Alex and me that he would be working a double, and Danny had a project to present that day, so neither of them would be around.

They had made a late reservation at some restaurant on Fourth Avenue. Alex and I were to bus up there after shopping with our birthday money and join them for dinner. We were kind of bummed, but hey, we all needed to work, as money was always a little tight.

Our birthday fell on Saturday this year, yay! Day of, Alex and I slept in until 11:00 am. We almost always woke up at the same time. Sharing the womb had put us on the same schedule. A note had been left; Ace reminding us to be at the Topanga Cafe at 8:00 pm.

"I thought they may have been pulling our leg. I thought we'd find a pony in the kitchen, or maybe Adam all wrapped up in ribbon." Alex snorted in amusement. "but I guess they were serious and we're on our own for the day."

"Well then, sis, let us go and shop."

It was a beautiful day, and we decided on a walk to Pacific Center Mall. Alex wanted new jeans and something cool to wear for his gigs. I wanted new clothes, too, and it was a unanimous decision to start at Le Chateau. They were a fairly new store and had the funkiest clothes.

We had a blast trying on the weirdest stuff we could find. Striped balloon pants, three-quarter elf boots, studded belts, and I tried on hoop earrings that were almost as large as my head. I ended up purchasing a white cotton dress that was snug, right down to the hips, and then flared out into a full skirt.

I looked really hot in it. Well, Alex said I did, and he never said anything that wasn't true. To go with the dress, I bought soft pink, pastel pumps and little pink tutu earrings, and a pastel pink, two-inch-wide hip belt, which thankfully gave length to my short waist. Alex bought black leather pants and a black pirate shirt; he looked really hot.

We had worked up an appetite and decided to go and get some chow before continuing our shopping. We sat in the food fair munching away when, who should show up, but Chrissie and Ralph.

"Hey guys, what's up?" Alex asked, eyeing up Ralph. "I thought you were grounded, Masters," he said, dryly. Looking a bit put out that Ralph was with his girlfriend.

"I was, but I told my mom it was yours and Mo's birthday. She let me off, so I called Chrissie and told her we should come down here and hang with you guys."

"Look at the cool stuff we got." I said, my subtle way of changing the subject. We pulled everything out and showed off our purchases. Chrissie said she couldn't wait to see Alex in his leathers.

"We come bearing gifts," Chrissie said, handing a box to Alex. She was almost vibrating as Alex unwrapped his birthday present and found the funkiest shoes ever. She had bought them at Fluevog on Granville Street. They were pointy and covered in different hues of blue that appeared to change to green when the lighting shifted. Fluevog was the most in place to get shoes from and I could tell from his expression that Alex was thrilled.

"I'm never taking them off," Alex said, and tugged Chrissie off her chair and onto his lap for a smoking hot kiss. I wanted to gag, when she gave him her signature starry eyes look that almost always happened after he kissed her.

I watched the look on her face and the soft expression in her eyes as they drew apart. She was very in love with my brother, and it made my heart glad to see him loved so completely by another.

Glancing quickly to his face before the moment was gone. I saw her expression reflected back from his eyes. Their fondness and love for each other seemed to have an eternalness to it that I had not witnessed with any of my brothers before, with the exception of Ace who looked that way at Kristine. It struck me then that if Alex and Chrissie ever broke up I'd be hit with a double whammy of helping them both get through it.

Chrissie handed me a box similar in size to Alex's. Inside were pointed wrestling shoes that looked just like Alex's, only with pearl white and pink, and a small stripe of blue that matched one of the blue hues in his. I tried them on, and they fit perfectly.

"I thought you guys would look really cool with similar shoes that are different enough to show off your individuality, but close enough to show your similar tastes in fashion."

"Thanks Chrissie," I said. "Clearly you spent a lot of thought and money on these gifts," I leaned over and hugged her.

"My turn." Ralph handed Alex a package then sat back, a look of anticipation on his face. Alex and Ralph had been best buddies since they were six years old. I had spent a lot of time around Ralph, but not much time outside of the circle, and didn't expect a gift from him, but happily watched as Alex opened his. Inside a box was an envelope. Inside the envelope was a coupon for Long and Mcquaid, Alex's favourite music store.

A big grin broke over Alex's face and he gave Ralph a hug. With Chrissie still on his lap, it was an awkward one arm thing.

"Here, Montana, this is for you." Ralph handed me a jewelry box. I was kinda shocked but managed to say thank you before I tore off the ribbon holding the top and bottom together.

Inside the box was a 10-karat gold astrological pendant and chain. The pendant was delicately carved and my first piece of real jewelry. With the necklace was a piece of paper. I opened it with shaking hands... it was a letter from Ralph.

Montana,

You and I have been friends since grade one, and ever since we played boys chase the girls at recess, and I accidentally stepped on the heel of your shoe, and you went skidding down the concrete on your knees and ended up with stitches, I've wanted to be your boyfriend. Your cute dimples and mischievous grin are enchanting and promise any guy lucky enough to kiss you fun and adventure. I love being around you, feeling your cool energy.

You have always had older boyfriends with cars and jobs. You always seemed out of my league. But now we seem closer to the same level with the band finally making money.

Here and now with this necklace, I humbly ask that you say yes to my proposal of being your boyfriend. If your answer is yes, then please take the necklace out of the box and put it on.

If not, then put the box away in your purse and that will be the end of it.

Love Ralph, your devoted and lovesick paramour

I looked up to see three faces peering back at me. One was curious, one was gleeful and one was hopeful. The middle one was Chrissie. Ralph must have asked her for help in choosing the gift and how to approach me. Smart really because she knew I liked things different, not your typical "hey wanna go out," and Ralph had scored with his thoughtful approach.

I took my time studying Ralph and seeing what I hadn't really noticed before. He was almost as tall as Alex, with brown hair and green eyes, and a slight olive complexion. Somewhere in his ancestry there must have been some Greek influence.

He'd taken me by surprise and the question remained, should I date my brother's best friend? There were definitely reasons not to but then my gaze fell on Alex and Chrissie. Things had worked out really well for them and she was my best friend. My earlier thoughts on possible complications down the road fell away. It was my birthday and I was in a great mood, one where throwing caution to the wind seemed like the right thing.

I slowly removed the necklace from the box and attached the chain around my neck. Ralph leaned forward and gave me a kiss. The first one ever and it wasn't bad. In fact it was a very, very good kiss, one that sent waves through my belly.

"Great letter," I whispered when he released my lips.

"Okay, what did I miss?" Alex asked.

I handed Alex the letter and leaned in to Ralph for another kiss. If I had known he could kiss like that, I would have let him kiss me back in grade one instead of punching him in the nose when he tried.

Alex scanned the letter, folded it and handed it back to me. He didn't say anything, and his expression gave nothing away as to his feelings regarding his sister and best friend dating.

"It is getting late. We need to go," I stood reluctantly. Ralph and Chrissie walked with us until we parted ways a block from our house. When we reached our porch Alex finally broke the silence. "What's going on?"

"What do you mean? He asked, and I accepted. Guess we'll double date now eh, bro?"

"I know all that," Alex said impatiently. "What I mean is why. Why did you accept?"

"To be honest, Alex, I had no idea that Ralph had feelings for me. Like thanks for never telling me. Anyway, I had never thought of him in terms of a boyfriend. But when I read that letter, it felt genuine and romantic and I have to give him credit for his creative approach. I figured we could have some fun together. I've been single for a while. I need to get back in the dating scene, and, well, it felt right. Is that a problem?"

"The problem, dear sister, is this; he is in love with you and always has been. I don't think it's fair for you to go out with him, if you don't feel the same way about him. Which," he held up his hand to stop me from interrupting, "I know you don't. Also, think of the impact on the band when you two break up it would get weird. And lastly, you gave this what, an entire thirty seconds before you said yes? Which means you're being impulsive instead of making a choice, and every time you do that, things turn out badly."

He had a point, but I wasn't about to let him guilt me into changing my mind. "Alex, why don't you lighten up? I mean, what about Chrissie? She has loved you since the third grade. She is totally in love with you. You never showed any interest in her until the Halloween dance, so why is it okay for you and not for me?"

"Because, Montana, I am not harboring feelings for anyone else, that's why. You are. You are in love with Adam."

That took me by surprise, and I stopped to ponder his words for a moment.

I definitely had feelings, but in love? I barely knew Adam. How could I be in love with someone I hardly knew? "Yes, I do have feelings for Adam. He stimulates me in ways I can't even explain. He shows me a different kind of life, one that's filled with magic, passion, art and a lifestyle most only dream of. I am too young, however, and I've been warned off thinking anything could ever happen between me and him. In the meantime, I have a life to live. Am I supposed to stay home and pine away? Don't I deserve to have fun?"

"I get what you're saying," he finally responded, "and I won't interfere. Just remember, if something goes wrong, he will be heartbroken. I don't mean to sound selfish, Montana, but if that happens, it also affects the band so be careful, okay, and tread lightly."

"Alex, it is not my intention to hurt Ralph or anyone else. Stop stressing, okay? I mean it's our birthday, let's go and have some fun!"

He laughed, and then we went our separate ways to get ready. The phone rang as I walked down the hall to my room. "I'll get it!" I yelled and nearly had to beat Alex off as I pulled the phone off the cradle. "Hello?"

"Hey brat, are you having a good birthday?" Dad's voice was crackly with the terrible connection.

"Dad! I can barely hear you! Yes, Alex and I are having a great time. Ace has planned something, we're about to leave." I wasn't about to go into details.

"Happy birthday, Peanut. Stay out of trouble. Put your brother on."

I said my goodbyes and passed the phone to Alex, who was practically levitating by this time. He laughed and joked for a couple of minutes, said, "I will," and that was that. He told me Dad was working doubles and had made a special effort to reach us.

Our bus ride to the restaurant was uneventful. We arrived five minutes early and found the door to the restaurant locked and the lights off. We thought about leaving but had no way of getting a hold of Danny or Ace to let them know we had come and gone, so we sat down to wait on the bus stop bench for the guys.

They arrived a few minutes later, and whistled at us.

"Aw, come on you guys," Alex said. "Cut that out."

"You two look amazing and a lot older than sixteen. We'll have to start locking Montana up." he said with a laugh. I blushed and stuck out my tongue at him.

"Honestly, Mo, I don't think I've seen you in anything but jeans and your cheerleading gear. You look very beautiful. Sexy too, which is disturbing. Seriously Ace, can we lock her up?" Ace laughed and clapped Danny on the back.

"As if, but if that's how you feel, you can be my dinner date, Dan, and regale me with stories of my beauty." I said.

"Yeah but probably not here." Alex gazed at the closed sign meaningfully. "Is there a particular reason why you numbskulls chose a closed restaurant?" Ace pulled a key out of his pocket and dangled it in front of Alex. Wearing a smirk, he unlocked the door to the darkened restaurant.

"What the? Although I'm impressed you have a key to a closed restaurant, what are we going to do now, cook our own dinner?" Alex sounded really sarcastic, his voice echoing in the darkness.

Danny reached around me and flipped on the lights to the restaurant.

"Surprise!"

I nearly toppled over in my three-inch heels. Danny's hand shot out and grabbed my elbow, stabilizing me. Holy hell! There must have been a hundred people crammed into the tiny restaurant. A stage was set with our equipment on it and above was a huge banner. "HAPPY BIRTHDAY, ALEX AND MONTANA."

Along the back wall was a buffet, set with every type of Mexican dish one could think of. Alex and I were bewildered. My first thought was, can we afford this? Ace must have read my mind.

He pulled Alex and me aside. "Dad asked me to roll out the red carpet. He sent some money and told me to say he is proud of you two and how hard you've been working, but now it's time to celebrate."

I thought of our conversation with dad earlier. This was why he'd been working double shifts, to pay for me and Alex to have an amazing birthday and told us that they had done this for us, because we had been working so hard. It was our time to relax and have fun with our friends.

"We owe it to dad to have a good time," Alex interrupted my thoughts. He was right, as I'd just come to a similar conclusion.

"You're right." I was at risk of shedding a few tears but quickly shut that down and worked the room with my twin. Ralph and Chrissie waited until the end, when they embraced us.

I can't speak for Alex, but I think he would agree when I say it was the best birthday ever. We ate amazing food, goofed off and laughed more than either of us had in a long time. Alex and the guys played an hour-long set to thunderous applause, of course.

The first song of the set was a waltz and Ace asked me to dance. We had never had a waltz together, but as my surrogate dad it seemed appropriate. While we danced, we talked about the day, where we had shopped, and what we had done to stay busy until meeting for dinner.

The tone of the night had me feeling equal with everyone in the room, instead of everyone having roles to play; we were just people out for a good time. Feeling emboldened, I told Ace about Ralph and Chrissie meeting us at the mall and about the gifts and the letter from Ralph. I laughed when he told me that he had already warned Ralph to keep his hands to himself.

I even told him about what Alex had said and his particular concern regarding the shelf life of the band if something negative should happen between Ralph and me. He seemed to contemplate that for a moment. His response was surprisingly nonchalant for Ace. He said that we would cross that bridge if and when we came to it.

On the next waltz, Danny asked me to dance, and he asked me about Adam.

"Are you disappointed, Mo, that Adam isn't here?"

I sighed. "Yes, the truth is I have a total crush on Adam and have since the first time we met, which isn't when you think, by the way." Yet again feeling emboldened, I confessed to Dan about the movie night and the drive home, with Adam. He laughed.

"Really? You think I didn't know? When I heard you and Eddy doing your story with Ace, it was all I could do to not give you up, I was laughing so hard. Adam had already phoned and told me before Eddy walked through the door. And by the way, the whole world can see perfectly that you have Adam on the brain; no secret there. I am surprised you agreed to date Ralph. Alex told me about it while you were dancing with Ace."

I took a moment to process that.

"My feelings aren't the problem, Dan, Adam's are. I don't know how he feels about me. I'm old enough to notice the age gap, and I don't think it's a big deal. I mean, I dated Matt, and Adam is only two years older than that. I don't like sharing this with you, as you're his best friend, but he and I have a special connection."

"So, in the meantime, you have Ralph to what, fill in the blanks, not be alone? What is your motivation exactly?"

"All those things, I guess," I sighed. "But hey, don't worry. Truth is, I enjoy Ralph, and I had no idea he was interested in me. I feel we could have fun together, and I don't think there is anything wrong with that. Is there anything wrong with that?"

"Of course not, Mo. I just wanted to check, and it wasn't Ralph I'm worried about, it's you."

"Well, if Adam is still around when I'm old enough to be deemed fit to have him," I grinned, "then I'm all over it. He and I will be together one day. You and Ace will have to come to terms with it. I've had glimpses of a future Montana and a future Adam, and they are together."

Danny laughed and said he would let Adam know. After the band finished playing, the party wound down. The four of us were the last ones to leave and drove home together. I was sound asleep when we arrived home. Ace carried me in and deposited me on my bed. The last conscious thought I remembered was the delicious goodbye kiss Ralph gave me just before he left.

Chapter 15

November 1981

In my dreamless drifting state, I relived that evening all over again. Everyone that mattered but Dad had been in attendance. Well, and Adam of course. The evening was as it should have been and I was very, very happy, but my newfound happiness was to be short-lived.

I was getting closer to events that I did not wish to relive. I felt this rather than knew it as a disturbance deep in my psyche. I needed to let go of this life—the events that had brought me to the pictures—I needed to sink into darkness. This was preferable to the pain and the torment of things I didn't want to experience ever again.

I had the choice, and the time was now. My physical connection severed and somewhere close I heard the flatline of a heart rate monitor that said I was dead. Finally, it's over.

I felt a jolt in my body that was so strong, my body felt lifted. Another jolt and I felt my body arch toward heaven. I didn't know if I was under attack or if I was ascending. I was hovering above the bed looking down at a pathetic form partially covered by a white sheet. A female form, her complexion as white as her gown and the sheets and the walls which contained her.

Then, I saw my brothers gathered around the form. Alex was talking urgently and holding both hands of the female in the bed. There was something very familiar about that lump in the bed. I moved closer to take a better look, my curiosity spurring me on. I recognized the shape; that shape was me. Before I could flee. I froze where I was shocked to see what I'd become. The shock increased when Alex looked directly into my eyes. He could see me? I was so startled, I didn't move.

"There you are," he said as he reached out to touch me. Suddenly, I crashed into my body. Just before I surrendered to the darkness I heard Alex's voice, and then nothing.

May 1981

Life was awesome for the first time in a long time. It seemed life was working in my favour for a change. Mercy and her crew stayed away from me and my friends, just like Eddy said she would. Alex had Chrissie, Otter had Kim, and I had Ralph. Band practice was out of control most days with us girls playing tricks on the guys. My personal favourite was hiding the drumsticks. Ralph would be desperately looking for his sticks just as the band would start up. He would alternate between tickling me and threatening to smack my butt until I would give in.

Sometimes I would loosen the snare drum. Ralph would hit it, and the drum would tilt or completely fall off. I would be running and laughing and he would be swearing and giving chase. All good fun—well, the girls thought so. For the guys it took a while, but when they finally realized we weren't going to stop, they joined in the game. We would find our cheerleading gear gone from our lockers at school. One time they pulled the pom-poms apart so they had to be restuffed. Another time after a game, our clothes went missing.

It wasn't all fun and games though. Ralph began the painful process of teaching me how to play drums. I say painful, because I was such a brat and felt sorry for anyone trying to teach me anything.

"Why?" I asked for the hundredth time.

"Girl drummers are so popular, and besides that, Montana, you have a natural rhythm. You'll love it."

I grumbled but did my best to follow his instructions. It gave us more time together outside of the circle which didn't happen much. For an hour after practice was done, he'd teach me, going through basic riffs and then our songs starting with the simplest ones.

He was right, of course. I did have a natural knack for it. All four of us Stanford kids had all taken lessons of some sort while Mom was alive. I never felt connected to an instrument, though, so it was easy to give up after she died. Alex was the only one who stuck to it.

One day, during a rehearsal for an upcoming gig, the girls and I hung out in the kitchen discussing our relationships. "You and Otter have so much fun together Kim, do you think he's end game?" Chrissie wiggled her eyebrows and we broke out into peals of laughter.

"No. I'm not into anything serious. We're way too young for that. I'm just having fun, enjoying high school best I can. What about you and Alex?" Her gaze shifted to Chrissie.

"As if! She's so in love with my brother it's almost sickening." Chrissie giggled.

"It's true, I am totally in love with Alex."

I was just about to share my thoughts and feelings on my relationship with Ralph, when he entered the kitchen to say he had something to show me. He told me to close my eyes and took me by the hand and led us into the garage.

"Open."

The first thing I saw was two sets of drums.

"Uh Ralph, why do you need two sets of drums?"

"They're not for me, Montana." he said laughing. "That second set is for you."

My shocked expression must have said it all because everyone laughed.

"Look, you have the potential to be a really good player, and I thought it was time you started practicing with us. It's the fastest way to improve. Alex and Otter said it was okay."

I walked over to my kit and ran my hands over it. The kit was pearl white with silver trim. The same make as Ralph's, Ayotte, only his set was black. He said no decent drummer should play on anything but Ayotte drums. I didn't know what to say.

My passion was to write poetry, music. I knew I had a stage presence as it came across in my dancing and cheerleading, but I did not consider myself a performer. I had not considered being part of a band in the capacity of a player, only as a writer.

Still, the pristine beauty of the drum set called to me and I was overwhelmed by the desire to try them out.

"Go ahead, Mo, and give them a try. It's already tuned."

I sat down on the stool, and felt very self-conscious. The girls and the guys waited for me to start. The only person I had played in front of was Ralph. He must have noticed my nerves as he sat down on his stool and picked out a riff for us to play together. We played exactly the same, right on cue and with perfect timing. The gang clapped when we were done, and I stood up and gave a theatrical bow.

"Not bad for an amateur," Alex said.

"Jerk," I said as I threw my sticks at him.

"Thanks, Ralph, you're the best," I said as I threw my arms around him.

"No more practical jokes?"

"Seriously? You're buying my obedience with a set of drums? I can only agree to try."

"Deal." he said and everyone laughed. The guys invited me to play with them for the remaining rehearsal time and when we were done, headed inside the house where I thought to properly thank him for the expensive gift. We were joined in the kitchen a few minutes later by the other four.

"Masters," Alex said when he saw us, "look what you've started. Chrissie and Kim both want to learn how to play an instrument."

Ralph and I laughed at the exasperated look on both Alex's and Otter's faces.

"Girls," Alex was explaining, "Montana lives here. If she wants to have band equipment in the garage, that's her prerogative. All us humble musicians can do is give you two some basic instruction. If you show some talent, then maybe you can start a band of your own down the road. If you prove to have no talent, then instruction time is over and no arguments. Do you both agree?"

The girls agreed to Alex's terms, and that was that. When Ace and Danny arrived home, I dragged them out to the garage to see my new drums. They had never heard me play, and they asked us to play a song. We played the song that the riff from earlier was a part of, this time without Ralph.

Without him, playing the music was different. Alex and I somehow connected, and our mutual connection grew with the song. And somewhere in there, I picked up on Otter as well, though more faintly. Sounds odd, I know, but I can't think of another way to describe the experience.

Feeling inspired at the end of the song, I flowed right into a solo that was not part of the song. That surprised everyone, self-included. When I was done, they clapped and congratulated me on my playing and Ralph amused them with tales of turning a brat into a drummer.

The guys stood around gabbing, and I left to go and make dinner, as it was my night. I felt elated! A whole new world had opened up to me. The drums had moved from an interest to a resonation deep inside, like a guitar string being plucked, and included in the resonation was Alex, and to a lesser extent, Otter.

I contemplated this new sensation, and when my brothers sat down to dinner, I was grinning from ear to ear. I pictured myself on stage with a huge crowd around me calling my name. *"Mon-tan-a, Mon-tan-a."*

"Montana? Montana, like hello."

Oops.

"Listen, Mo," Ace began. "What do you plan on doing with this drumming thing? What I mean is, isn't one musician in the family enough?"

I looked into Ace's eyes, looking to see if this was a joke... he looked serious. I thought he was an ass for asking. Like seriously, I just finished my first time playing and already he was on my case.

"To be honest, Ace, I never thought about music as a career choice before today. Well, not playing, anyway, perhaps writing." I tried making a joke, by adding it was my way of torturing Ralph but they didn't laugh.

"We, meaning Dan and I, wanted to check. I don't know how thrilled Dad would be to hear his little girl, his only girl, was running around town, hanging out in clubs and getting ogled by older guys."

"Ace, right now the band has a drummer, and as far as I know, he has no intention of leaving. I have no time to start a band of my own, and I don't really have the inclination either. If I ever wish to play, and the location seems questionable, I'll check with you first." It was a bold move, basically saying it was my choice but I was open to hearing their opinion on locations, but as they seemed satisfied the topic shifted to other things.

I silently thanked Eddy, as he had been giving me how-to-communicate-with-Ace lessons for a while now and tonight it had paid off.

The next day, Chrissie, Kim and I received a party invitation to join our new friends on the West Side. The guys had not met them yet, as they always had a gig when we went, but this time they didn't and opted to come with us.

Shelley's parents were out of town, so the party was at her house. She opened the door when we arrived and fixed her gaze on Alex. Great. Why did all the girls fall for my quiet, not-interested brother? Poor Chrissie, she saw it too, and sent me a look of exasperation that said, will it ever end?

After the awkward moment, Shelley offered to make some introductions. She promptly linked her arm through Alex's, and expected the rest of us to follow behind like we were their personal harem or something. Chrissie cut off from the group to say hi to Dave and Ben, and I took Ralph to meet Cole.

They recognized each other from playing. Cole had a band of his own, so they talked shop while I kept my eye on Alex. I saw him glance constantly at Chrissie; he was giving her the signal to rescue him from a conversation that he obviously didn't want to be a part of, but she kept ignoring him. She ignored his silent plea for help. I excused myself and made my way over to her.

"What's up? Why are you ignoring my brother?"

"Your brother's a big boy; he can take care of himself," she answered with a hiss.

I couldn't remember a time when I had seen her in such a snit. She turned her back on me, and her attention back to Dave and Ben, and I went over to rescue Alex. He was at the centre of a group of girls, some of which I recognized, like Leigh, affectionately known as a bit of a slut. No shaming she used the term herself and owned it and didn't give a crap about having a bad reputation. She was slipping a piece of paper into my brother's pocket. I sidled up to him and pulled it out of his pocket, handing it back to her.

"Sorry, Leigh," I said with regret in my voice. "He won't be needing your number. He's taken, remember?" I laughed, making light of this encounter more as a joke than the warning it truly was, and hoped she would get the point. Taking Alex by the arm, I said I had someone for him to meet and took him over to Cole and Ralph.

Alex caught up on the conversation and the three of them really hit it off and seemed to speak the same language.

"Montana plays drums as well, Cole, if you ever need a drummer."

Ralph smiled at me as he said this, grabbing my hand and pulling me into an embrace.

"Yeah, Ralph. Mo can play, but she won't be, not next weekend or any other time," Alex said in a deadpan voice.

"Why not?" Ralph asked suspiciously. "We're already booked next weekend, and they're looking for a fill-in for their drummer. Either that, or she could fill in for me and I could play with them?"

Ralph had not been part of the conversation in the kitchen with Ace and Danny regarding a music career being a bad choice for the family's only female.

"Um, would like to say something," I began, but was rudely cut off.

"You don't get a say, Mo," Alex said quietly. "I said no, and that's final."

I don't know who was more shocked, Alex for saying it, or Ralph and myself... it had to be a joke. We were twins - the same age; he had no authority over me in any way.

"Okay, Alex, no more joking," I said with a giggle.

He turned around and walked out the door. I went to follow, but Ralph told me to stay. He wanted to talk to Alex, to find out what was going on.

"Alex, hold up. What the hell's wrong with you? Are you jealous of your own sister?"

Alex said nothing, just turned around and walked down the driveway. Ralph came back inside and said he thought Alex was jealous of me but didn't say anything more. An hour or two passed, and we decided to leave. Neither of us was in the partying mood, and the rest of the gang seemed to sense this, so they came as well.

My thoughts were on my brother. I could sense his turmoil, and it bothered me. I never felt turmoil from Alex, although I knew he had with me on many occasions. When we got on the bus, Alex was already on it. He was sitting in the back row, legs up, ankles crossed, eyes closed. We sat at a respectful distance to give him his space.

I felt responsible for this little rift between Ralph and Alex, while also not understanding it. I excused myself and went to talk to Alex.

"Alex I don't know what happened, but I feel responsible."

He smiled at me, and I knew everything was fine between us. Whatever was going on, it was between him and Ralph. As I gazed into his eyes, I saw his thoughts in the way he'd always been able to do with me.

I knew what had happened. I could see it like he had just spoken the words. Ralph and I—his best friend and his twin sister—had stood against him. Well, not really, but that was how he chose to look at it, or more accurately, react to it. Alex was the leader of the band and had witnessed Ralph challenging that in front of another leader from another band. The issue was never about the drums; it was about loyalty. I had taken the one thing from him that he could do, loved to do.

He had tested us, and we had come up short. We chose what we thought, which was opposed to what he thought. Now I needed to explain it in such a way that maybe Alex could forgive, or Ralph could apologize?

I went back to my seat. "Ralph, would you talk to Alex?" He frowned in response.

I explained to Ralph and asked him to be the bigger man. He rose from his seat; went to the back of the bus, and sat with Alex. They were deep in conversation for the rest of the bus ride, and I relaxed back in my seat after I was sure they weren't going to fight.

My thoughts drifted to Chrissie and her mood tonight. She was silent all the way home and talked to no one. Tomorrow, I will find out what her problem is and fix it. That was the least I could do to prove my loyalty to my brother.

I smiled to myself as I rehearsed what I would say to her in the morning. I hoped it would go as well as my meddling with Ralph and Alex had.

Chapter 16

November 1981

I can honestly say that remembering those times with my friends and brother was like a calm before the storm. We had fun and we were all together, but things would change. I would change and not all change is good.

May 1981

The next morning, I met Chrissie for breakfast at McDonald's on Robson Street. She was still in a bad mood, but at least she wasn't snotty like she had been the night before. We sat by the window with our sausage and pancakes. I watched while she covered her food in so much syrup that everything was swimming.

"What's going on with you? Why did you do that to Alex last night? Do you know how much you hurt him?"

"I just can't do it anymore, Mo." That was not what I was expecting. A tear slid down her cheek and she slapped it angrily away.

"It's the popularity thing, Montana. It's driving me nuts! Everywhere we go, someone stops us, usually a girl. They sidle up to him or ogle him, or—or proposition him right in front of me."

I tried not to laugh aloud as this was clearly an issue for her, but I knew my brother and there was no way in hell he'd ever cheat on Chrissie. "Alex doesn't give a damn about any of the girls that approach him for any reason, unless they have a recording contract in their hand. His eyes and heart are yours, and yours only. Come on, you know that's true."

I expected her to agree with me but she didn't, instead she took a bite of food and chewed slowly like she was contemplating her response. "It's just that, Mo. I did think long and hard about what would happen if he got popular and was sure I could go along for the ride. Hang on to his coat tail, but the truth is, I just want to be going out on a date. I want to be able to go out with some guy, and it's just him and me, not us and the band, or us and the world. Do you understand? I have to break up with him, Mo. There is nothing else I can do."

"You are saying you love my brother but not his life?" I couldn't pretend that I didn't know what she was talking about. Alex and the band's popularity in general was growing. Things would only increase as time went on, and if they got a recording contract, things would increase a hundred fold or more. She would never ask him to pick her over the band.

I kinda felt stupid for not seeing the situation earlier. I knew what kind of person Chrissie was and felt she knew the price of dating a local, minor celebrity but she was right. It was better to get out now, before the big leagues and before their relationship went deeper. Chrissie had been Alex's first girlfriend, his first love and he would be devastated by this.

"That is exactly what I'm saying." She swiped another tear from her face but there was no anger in her movement this time.

"I understand, really I do and you've obviously given this a lot of thought. Are you sure I can't talk you out of it?"

"No, I have decided. It is better to face things now than down the road. Please tell me this won't affect our friendship, Montana."

I sighed, hating this, but what could I do? "Of course not. Friends for life right? Aren't we blood sisters after all?"

She giggled. "Yes, we are."

I stood up. "You'll tell him soon?"

"I will." She stood too, and we hugged before I said goodbye and headed for home. I joined the guys in the garage for some play time, needing the anxiety release the drums offered me. When they were done, I prepared to begin my lesson with Ralph but he said he had to leave. I got ready to leave also, but the guys weren't ready to end rehearsal, so they asked me to fill in for Ralph.

Playing with them was a lot harder than jamming or doing warm-up drills. I felt awkward and silently agreed with

Alex that I wasn't ready for the big league yet. We played for an hour and were calling it quits when Chrissie arrived and asked Alex to speak with him privately.

They left for a walk, and Otter and I went into the house to have lunch. When Alex arrived home, he went directly to his room and closed the door. I knew what had gone down, and left him alone to think. Otter gave me a shrug and left a few minutes later.

When Ace and Danny got home later that day, I told them Alex had seemed upset after practice and had been in his room all afternoon. I didn't tell them I knew why he was upset, as that would be betraying Chrissie's trust.

Ace knocked on Alex's door, and after getting no response, opened his door. He'd left a note on his bed stand. "Back later."

"I'll speak with him when he returns." Ace said and went to shower and clean up from work.

Over dinner, Danny shared with Ace and me a letter he'd received from Paris. An art dealer friend he'd made in New York, Katya, was coming to Vancouver for a few weeks to coordinate an art exhibit of the Impressionists, on loan from the Louvre and other private collectors.

"When is she coming in, little brother?" Ace asked.

"End of June, right when school is ending, so it shouldn't disrupt exams for the brats," Danny grinned at me.

"Good timing. It won't disrupt another visit. I heard from Dad today, and he's home in July for your nineteenth birthday, Dan."

Danny lit up with the news, so did I, and for a moment, Alex and his problems were forgotten.

"Where will she sleep, Danny? Do you want her to bunk with me? Or I could bunk with Alex and she could have my room," I said excitedly.

"Thanks for the offer, baby girl, but I think I'll bunk with Alex, and she can have my room, assuming she wants to stay here. She may want to stay with Adam. He knows her and has a spare bedroom in his apartment, or maybe, as her costs are being covered, she will prefer a hotel. Too early to tell."

I could see Ace covertly gauging my reaction to what Dan had said regarding the possibility of his "friend" staying with Adam. I put on my nonchalant expression not wishing to give away how much it bothered me.

We were discussing possible plans when Alex walked in. Without saying a word to any of us, he headed straight for his room and shut the door. Ace excused himself to go and talk to Alex. While Danny and I cleared and washed the dishes, I asked him questions about Katya to pass the time.

When Ace joined us in the kitchen, we changed topics and asked what was up with Alex.

"Alex is processing a lot right now," Ace began. "Right before practice today, Ralph let him know he was leaving the band. Right after practice, Chrissie broke up with him."

"What! Are you serious? Why?"

"Why to which one of those? Alex thought he, Otter and Ralph would go all the way to the top together. This has really unsettled him, even more than Chrissie breaking up with him, I think he needs time to lick his wounds and decide what to do about the hole Ralph is leaving behind."

I took that in, and thoughts whirled around in my mind. He couldn't just leave. How could he just leave and why didn't he tell me? I needed to speak with Ralph and see if I could change his mind, or at least give him a piece of my mind.

His brother answered the door when I arrived, and let me in. Ralph was in his room with the door closed. I didn't knock, just stormed in. I stood with hands on hips and demanded to know what was going on.

"Montana, it's not what you think," he began. "I'm leaving the band and joining Cole's because we're moving. Not because of any animosity between Alex and me."

More shocking news. He was leaving not just the band but his life here, and me. He started to talk again, but I'd heard enough. I slapped his face and turned around and left. We were through! The guy didn't even have the guts to be honest with me.

He had obviously known for a while and thought he could just slide in all these bloody life-changing events that affected me and my brother and stroll away like no feelings were hurt. Well, screw him. My emotions swelled and brewed like a hurricane as I stormed off.

The next day was Monday. Alex and I were silent on the way to school. Trying to hold back the tide of emotions and remain calm for my brother's sake was the hardest thing. I needed to, in order to prepare myself to be around Ralph, and I felt that Alex was doing the same.

He stopped at the smoke pit to talk with Otter. Inside I passed Chrissie at her locker talking to some grade ten guy who was newer to the school. I nodded my head and kept walking to my locker.

My heart was racing when I opened the door, and leaned my forehead against the cold metal. "Just breathe." Images of Chrissie and Alex together assaulted me and a feeling of utter betrayal filled me. First she breaks Alex's heart and now she's already flirting? Like seriously, I really thought they'd be end-game. My heart was just starting to slow down when Ralph suddenly appeared and said he needed to talk to me.

"I have nothing to say to you, Masters. You're leaving school, the band, and me. Seems pretty clear. You have obviously known for a while and chose not to tell me or Alex. I have zero respect for the way you chose to lay this on us and on the same day that Chrissie broke up with Alex. What a shit friend you've turned out to be." He grabbed me as I turned to walk away.

"Wait, what? I had no idea Chrissie broke up with Alex," He gripped my shoulders. "but this doesn't mean I'm leaving you, Montana." He pulled me into a tight embrace. "I'm not leaving you," he repeated against the shell of my ear. "Yes, I am leaving the band and the school. I am not, however, leaving you or my friends."

He had my attention.

"Remember my grandfather died last year,?"

I nodded.

"He left money for my brother and me, for our education. All I want is music, and my parents have reconciled themselves to that. But they don't want me to graduate and only have the band. We've decided to use my part of the inheritance for a performing arts school."

"My brother is attending university and the two schools are only a mile apart, about forty minutes from downtown. So, my parents made the decision to move to make the commute easier. Robert and Cole are just a few blocks from where our new house is. It made sense for me to take their offer and join their band. I'm sorry you didn't hear this from me directly. It was always my intention to tell you, but I knew you wouldn't take it well, so I held back. I love you, Mo, and I want us to still date. Can we?"

I told him to give me a few days. I needed time to think about all I had heard, and what it all meant. The future, which had seemed so secure yesterday, had suddenly changed. As I walked home from school that day, a deep sense of foreboding followed me and my instincts said things would get worse before they got better.

Ralph and I continued to date, although things were not the same, and seeing each other was very sporadic. He was immersed in what was coming and getting started with the new band. Otter and Alex continued with our band and I filled in as drummer until they found a new drummer. Alex's heart wasn't in it, and if they didn't find a replacement soon, the summer gigs would have to be canceled.

School was almost done for the year and life was changing rapidly and not in a way I liked. Cheerleading was done and summer holidays were fast approaching. This on its own was a reason to be happy, but with Chrissie busy flirting with older boys, including Eddy, and Otter and Kim calling it quits, and Ralph M.I.A, things felt really off.

One day at practice, Ralph made the suggestion that I replace him. Which, of course, had been his intention all along. Alex and I looked at each other and knew it wouldn't work. I tried making light of it by saying I should go and play for Cole's band and Ralph could stay, but no one laughed.

Tensions between Ralph and Alex, Ralph and me, and me and Chrissie. as well, were making me edgy, so when our West Side buddies set up a rumble against the East Side guys, excitement rippled through our little group.

A few times a year, the East Siders would sneak to the West Side and beat up a few people, kick them with their Dayton boots until some ribs were broken and then go slinking back to their hole on the East Side.

Us West Enders didn't like them coming onto our turf and messing with our people. Rumbles had happened in the past, and I knew for a fact that both Danny and Ace had participated. A crew of us decided to join them on this one.

Eddy, Alex, Chrissie and I went together—awkward—and we met the others there.

Chrissie wasn't fighting, but she would act as a lookout. We met up with our friends at the appointed time, just before dusk. The rumble was being held in the UBC bushes. A time-honored tradition. Gang fights had been happening there since our dad had been in high school.

The guys from the East Side were total greasers. They reminded me of characters from *The Outsiders*. No kidding, I thought I had stepped onto the pages of a Susie Hinton book.

I was the only girl from downtown to show up to fight... and only three girls from Lord Bying joined us.

Alex wanted me to stay in the back, but I told him I was a good fighter. I would pick a small guy to fight, not to worry. Eddy was beside me anyway, so I had nothing to fear. He could take on three guys and still win.

I was beginning to wonder when the fireworks would start, when I found myself on the ground with a knee pressed painfully on my back. The East Siders had decided to circle around and jump us from behind. Eddy pulled the guy off of me before fighting his way to the core of the war.

I kicked my attacker before he could get up and I gave him a few good kicks to the ribs and one to the head to knock him out. I could see Ralph was just ahead of me and had two guys on him. I joined in and grabbed the smaller one by the back of his collar and dragged him off.

Ralph looked up and gave me a brilliant smile and I could tell he was having fun. Hell, I was having fun, and grinned back. The guy I had hauled off Ralph moved quickly and I ducked in time to miss a blow to the head.

I managed to get an uppercut to his jaw, but it didn't slow the guy down. I looked for my bat. The rules were no blades for a rumble—we didn't want anyone dying—but girls, if any showed up, could use a bat or club. It was lying on the ground about twenty feet away from me. Damn, too far. I punched him again.

His return punch put me down, and then he was on top of me with his hands around my throat.

I was winded and there was no strength behind the punch I landed on his jaw. In retaliation, he kept one hand on my throat and punched with the other. I held my forearms over my face trying to block the worst of it. I was almost unconscious when his weight fell off of me. I looked up and saw Chrissie standing above me with the bat.

She was holding out her hand to help me up. All I could do was roll over, and cough before painfully climbing to my feet. If Chrissie hadn't been there, I hate to think what would have happened. There was to be no permanent damage, I don't know, maybe it was me, but death seemed like permanent damage. That was a startling thought, and with fear for the others, I moved ahead to rejoin the fighting when our guys started running back in our direction.

I grabbed Chrissie and the bat and ran for cover. It was the cops. Someone must have finked, or having seventy kids running around in the woods hadn't gone unnoticed. I didn't know where our guys were but I knew where they would be heading.

We crawled through the brush in the direction of the parked car. Just as we were breaching the tree line, we saw Eddy and Alex being detained by the police. I had to think of a way to get the guys off the hook. I looked over at Chrissie, and a plan formed in my mind.

"Montana, can't do that," she wailed.

"You have to, Chrissie. I look like I've been fighting, or I would do it. You're the only one who can pull this off. Now, go!" I commanded.

Chrissie raced down the tree line a bit, and exited a path about twenty feet away from the police.

"Excuse me, officers," she said, sounding upset and agitated. "There are two young boys in the bush, just up the path. They are getting beaten on by a few ruffians. Please, you must go help!"

The officers looked at their captives. They didn't have anything on them, and they knew it. They hadn't caught them doing anything but getting in a car. They could grill Alex about his fresh eye injury but capturing guys in the act of fighting would allow them to make legitimate charges.

They let go of Alex and Eddy and gave them a stern warning and then took off up the path that Chrissie had pointed out. I exited the bushes after the cops left. Farther down the path, Matt, Otter, Ralph and Dillon did the same.

We were laughing and congratulating Chrissie on her outstanding performance. I took a quick survey of the damage to our little group. Ralph had a cut above his eye and was bleeding badly. He would need stitches. Dillon had a bleeding lip. Alex had a black eye, and so did I. Matt's knuckles were bleeding, and his lip was cut.

Otter wasn't bleeding, but his ribs hurt awful bad, and he was having a hard time breathing. I couldn't talk, only whisper, as being choked had obviously done something to my vocal chords. Thank goodness it hadn't been Alex, as he was the lead singer.

Looking in the car mirror, I could see finger bruises around my throat. I had a blackeye, and the right side of my face was swollen and bruised. I looked the worst, but

Otter was doing the worst, so Eddy took everyone to the hospital after dropping Chrissie, Alex and me off at the house. Chrissie said goodbye, and Alex and I went inside.

Ace and Danny were both home when we got there. When they saw us, they almost knocked over the kitchen table in their haste to get up and come and see us up close.

"I know we look bad—" Alex began.

I cut in, "—but you should see the other guys!"

Alex rolled his eyes and said I wasn't helping and that, perhaps, I should just shut up. Dan bathed Alex's cut while we took turns telling the guys our story. There was lots of confusion, as Alex and I had different perspectives, as we were fighting in different places of the rumble. Ace and Danny listened with disapproving looks on their faces.

It turns out they all knew the guy who had his hands around my throat. I didn't say that I had almost lost consciousness, but I could tell Alex knew, as he gave me one of his twin looks that said he knew I was full of crap when I made light of the situation. When we finished our tale, they broke out in laughter, confusing the hell out of us.

"You two must think we're dumb or something," Ace said.

"Huh." Alex and I both responded with identical expressions.

"Don't do that," Danny said, laughing so hard he was silent with tears in the corners of his eyes.

"Don't do what?" Alex and I both asked. This time we all laughed.

"You two are so funny; the entire West End, well at least those under the age of twenty-five, knew what was going down tonight at UBC. When we saw you leave with Eddy, we knew exactly where you two brats were going."

"Are we in trouble?" I asked Ace.

"No, Mo, you guys are not in trouble. I knew you would go eventually, but that is your first and last rumble, understood?"

I argued with him that I was fine, and that I fought well. He knew I could fight, that wasn't a problem; the problem was he didn't like seeing me beat up. The neighbors were starting to wonder if he and Danny beat me.

"Well, what if I go but promise not to fight?" I asked.

Ace laughed, "Like I would ever believe you wouldn't. You couldn't help yourself. As soon as someone else was at a disadvantage, you would be in there. We don't need to make any decisions right now, but if another rumble happens while you are still a minor, we will talk about it then. Besides," he added with a twinkle, "I might want to come, too."

The next day at school, the rumours were flying. By the end of the day, Eddy had fought and killed ten guys, which was ridiculous, and Chrissie's story had been embellished, also. Those two were the heroes of the UBC war and would forever be remembered that way.

Chapter 17

November 1981

Somewhere in my psyche, I was smiling. My God, life seemed so simple... have some stress, duke it out. Next day, everything was okay. There was no way to insulate myself from the emotions that attached to every event in my life. I internalized everything. Was life on earth really the place for someone like me? I didn't think so, and hadn't thought so for quite some time.

June 1981

A few days after the rumble, school ended for the summer. Ralph and his family had moved the day after school ended, and other than Otter and Eddy, everyone seemed to go their separate ways. It was weird as I knew it would be. Like I get it, things can't always stay the same but this was more than just a shift, it was an emptiness that I didn't know what to do with.

Other activities came up to fill in the void of missing people. We did a big clean on the house, as Danny's friend Katya was due to arrive from Paris, and as usual, our house needed some attention.

Katya had agreed to stay at our house in Danny's bedroom, so I added some feminine touches. When Dan came in for the inspection, he stared wistfully at the linens I'd used instead of his basic plaid.

"Montana, where did you find the bedding?" he asked quietly.

"In the top of the linen closet. I thought the flowers would brighten up your otherwise very drab room and make it look pretty. You don't like it?"

"No, of course, I like it, it's not that, it's just... well... it was Mom's, and I haven't seen it since Dad packed up her stuff."

I wanted to ask him questions about her, but before I could, Ralph stuck his head in the doorway.

"Oh, there you are. I just came to get the rest of my equipment."

I walked into the garage with him. Alex was in there already, changing stuff around and putting my kit where Ralph's had sat.

"For auditions," he said, and then walked out to give us privacy.

Ralph and I didn't talk about it. I was pretty sure our relationship would be over once he was gone, intentionally or not. His brother was just loading the last of the sound system that Ralph had contributed to the band into his van. Ralph kissed me and got in the passenger seat, and waved as they pulled out and drove off. Both Alex and I returned the wave, but ours held nowhere near the enthusiasm that Ralph's had. He was beginning a new and exciting journey and we had been left behind. It stung but it was hard not to be happy for him. With heavy hearts, we went back into the house.

The next morning, Adam picked up Danny and they left for the airport to get Katya. With Ace at work and the house guest ready, Alex and I decided to get in some practice time.

"Alex, I was wondering if you would tell me why you're so opposed to me playing in the band?"

"Ralph asked me if I was jealous of you," he said with a grin. "It's hard to explain, but I'll try. One reason is you're good-looking, Montana. Hot, actually. I have my hands full fending off the fans already. I don't have the time or inclination to do the same for you. I'm there for me and to get into the groove, get into the energy of the music."

I'd never considered being mauled by fans as my experience hadn't taken me beyond the garage, but when I thought about Alex, all I saw was dreamy eyed fan girls.

"Wait! You're not suggesting that all your fan girls are going to maul me like they do you?"

Alex burst out laughing. "Maybe. But I was thinking more of the guys. That's not my only issue though. When you and I play together, I feel your energy and mine changes and aligns with yours. We already share everything; I wanted something of my own. Think of it like this, imagine me in your dance class and invading your energy. How would you feel?"

I imagined Alex in my class with his long lanky body in a pair of tights and couldn't help giggling.

"You're right, Alex, and I feel stupid that I didn't see that myself. It's different for me. I like it when our energies mingle. I feel as though we feed the music, and it gives us a sound that you didn't have with Ralph."

My brother's expression turned thoughtful. "You're right, it does seem to take on a life of its own. It's so powerful, I actually find it addictive. When you first began to rehearse with us, I assumed that energy would only happen at first and lessen with time, but quite the opposite is happening. It may be something I have to come to terms with, because you're really good, and I may need you."

Sure enough, Alex had created a self-fulfilling prophecy. He approached me a few days later to say he needed me.

"So listen up, Mo, the band has a gig next weekend. Ralph can't help us as he's already playing and it's coming up too fast to teach a new drummer all the songs they would need to know in time. Will you do the gig with us? Ralph said he could show up for our second set if need be, but we still need someone for the first set for sure."

I mulled over what he had just said. "Are you sure it's okay with Otter?"

"Otter would prefer you and wants you as the permanent drummer. It's me, and only me, having a challenge, and you know what my challenge is, but I'm running out of time and I need you. The band's need is greater than my personal feelings right now."

I was really excited. This was exactly what I had been praying would happen. I wanted the chance. I wanted to see if I was good enough.

"Okay, brother, I'll do it. But I want extra rehearsal time this week, deal?"

"Deal," he said with a sigh of relief.

We heard the car out front and hurried through the house and out to the front deck. Danny opened the passenger door of Adam's car and reached in his hand, assisting Katya in exiting the vehicle.

Funny, I had never seen him do that before. Holy crap! The girl was gorgeous! Alex and I stood gaping like a couple of Venus flytraps looking for lunch.

She was my height, but where I was all legs, she was all curves. She had jet-black hair and sparkling green eyes. When she smiled, her perfect white teeth gleamed in the sunlight and her laugh was like little bells.

Danny grabbed her bags and waved Adam off. He carried everything and escorted her up the steps. He introduced her and she spoke with a perfect Parisian accent. I bet this girl has broken a thousand hearts. Danny was completely engrossed by her. As I watched them exchange a few words, I saw him blush. Wow, Danny had actually blushed.

Give me a break. Her manners were as impeccable as her appearance. I figured Danny would propose marriage in three days flat! She eyed me up as she took my hand and said *enchanté*. I had never been this close to perfection, and I suddenly felt self-conscious about my looks.

I still had a black eye from the rumble, and I was wearing shorts and a t-shirt, no makeup, and I was sweaty from practicing drums. How humiliating. I bet Katya had never sweated a day in her life. I showed her into the house and to her room. She glided to the bathroom to freshen up and left me with orders regarding her luggage. It didn't even dawn on me to say no.

"Danny, why didn't you tell us about Katya? Look at me, I'm grunged out."

"Tell you what?" He looked confused. "Isn't this your regular look? Why would that change?"

"Oh, come now, like dur, the woman is gorgeous... I mean, holy crap, she looks like royalty, and I look like a peasant."

"You think she looks like royalty," he said with a sly smile. "There are many women in Paris that look exactly like her."

"You mean you're not infatuated with her? I was watching you, and you seemed smitten."

"We're only friends, Montana. I have never felt more for her than that. Why are you stressing about her appearance, compared to you?"

"Danny, look at me." I whined. "Compared to her, I'm an ugly duckling. I can't compete with perfection. Adam must be head over heels, and... Oh God! Is he one of the art friends coming over tonight?

He nodded his head.

"Danny, how could you?" I stormed off to my room to call Chrissie; it was going to take another female to understand my feelings. Chrissie didn't prove to be as helpful as I had hoped. She wanted to see Katya for herself, as she felt I was exaggerating.

When she arrived, she didn't even come in. She stood in the doorway and gawked. Katya got up to introduce herself, and seeing Chrissie's expression set a small cat grin of satisfaction upon Katya's lips.

"Eez veery neece to meet you, Krissy," Katya said as she extended her perfectly manicured, perfumed hand.

Chrissie mumbled something and then said she had to go. Hah, that's the last time she would tell me I was exaggerating. I laughed to myself. Ace and Kristine showed up next. They pulled a Chrissie and stopped dead in their tracks just inside the front door.

Katya gave Ace a long, appreciative look. When I introduced them, I made sure to say that Kristine was Ace's girlfriend, as his only response was to impersonate a guppie, moving his lips, but nothing was coming out. I also gave him a boot to wake him up from his trance. This was getting old fast.

Alex and I were cooking dinner but he was useless as he kept taking off to the living room to visit with Katya, Danny, Ace and Kristine. Then he would run into the kitchen to tell me something else I didn't know about her and what she liked to eat. Like I cared. Did our house suddenly become a restaurant? If my mom's famous fried chicken wasn't good enough for this girl then too bad!

A few minutes later, Kristine was in the kitchen. "What the heck is going on, does she shit rainbows or something?" I snorted with amusement.

"If Ace doesn't get that buttery smoochy look off his face I'll smack it off!" I watched as she stormed back into the living room and inserted herself on my brother's lap. This was one of those times when I really appreciated that our kitchen had a door.

After dinner and cleanup were done, Katya decided they needed to pick up some French wine and pastries to create a Parisian salon for the artsy get-together they were having later in the evening.

Danny and Katya left to buy the supplies she wanted. Ace and Kristine left for their movie and I took off over to Eddy's to hang out for the night. Pat was at Eddy's, and when I arrived, asked me what I thought of Dan's friend.

"Oh yeah, she arrived all right, and everything is just so enchanting," I said, rolling my eyes.

"Is there something wrong?"

"No, I just wanted to escape before they returned home from the store. They're all so taken with her that they've been no help whatsoever. It was Danny's night to cook. He had me and Alex do it. However, Alex spent all his time fawning over Katya. I did all the cleanup and dishes, too."

They laughed as I explained what had happened to everyone since Katya's arrival. When I was done whining, we walked to Second Beach to watch the sunset.

I preferred when the summer was over and the tourists had left. The locals respected the space; the tourists just saw another amazing beach, I guess. I didn't know really, as I had never been a tourist. I just noticed the difference.

Still, any time was a good time to congregate at the beach in the evening. We stopped for some Big Gulps along the way to add to our rum, yum! After hours of drinking and socializing, I felt I was ready to go home and face another round of Katya worship. Big mistake!

As soon as we got within three houses of my home we could hear the party.

"Brace yourselves," I said, as I opened up the front door. Our living room looked like a true Paris salon. Danny's work was on display. There were platters of French bread, with assorted cheeses and bowls of grapes.

Danny was wearing a French beanie that Katya had brought for him, and someone had drawn a mustache on him. With his striped shirt he looked like Gene Kelly in *An American in Paris*. The discussion seemed to be centred on the right type of model to use for sketching.

The three of us stood in our beachwear in the entrance feeling, and I'm sure looking, completely out of place. Without skipping a beat, Katya used me to illustrate her example. First, she listed all the physical attributes that I had to be a good artist model.

Size and shape of my breasts were okay, should be a little larger, a little too skinny, freckles were hard and could get in the way of the final copies... *blah, blah, blah...* was all I heard. I managed to blush through her tirade of my faults, particularly when she got onto specifics regarding my feminine parts.

Eddy found his tongue and saved me from her final barrage by interrupting and introducing himself. She immediately went to work on Eddy by trying to seduce him. Eddy, however, proved disinterested... haha... so she went to work on Pat next, and he fell in the first twenty seconds.

I suddenly felt tired. For days, there had been so much hype about Katya coming to visit and now that she was here, I was already done with her and wished she wasn't staying with us. I didn't belong in this crowd of people. I caught Adam eyeing me, but ignored him and whispered in Danny's ear that I was spending the night at Eddy's.

I didn't know if he had actually heard me or not, so I wrote a note for Ace and left it on the fridge. Eddy and I left and headed down to 7-11 to get some more Coke. I needed another drink. We took our pop back to his place and sat up yapping about this and that.

The next morning, I found Ace in the kitchen making coffee when I arrived home.

"Montana Stanford, where have you been? I have been worried sick!"

"You must be joking? I spent the night at Eddy's. I told Danny, and I also left you a note on the fridge."

Something else was going on here. Ace looked really angry, but he also looked really upset. Something had happened. I decided to try a diversion and change directions.

"What happened last night?" I asked. "Something is upsetting you."

He gave me a look that tore at my heart and then told me that he and Kristine had broken up last night. Aha! I bet they argued about Katya. That would not be cool to bring up.

Instead, I told him I was sorry it had happened. My empathy seemed to anger him, and he told me to clean up the kitchen.

"Now hold on a minute, I know exactly what's going on here. You've taught me this one. It's called transference. You're pissed off, probably at your own stupidity for slobbering all over Katya and pissing off your woman, so now you are taking it out on me. Well, forget it, bud. Alex and I made dinner last night. Then I did all the clearing and the dishes. This mess is from Danny's party and there's no way I am cleaning up after that simpering Barbie doll that everyone is so gaga over. Dan's friend—he can do it!"

"Montana, I don't care at this particular moment whose damn job it is. I just want it done. I gave you an order, and you will follow it. Clean it up, NOW!" He yelled the last bit as he grabbed my arm and shoved me over to the sink. I still had on my tennis shoes and he was barefoot.

I slammed down on his bare foot and took off at a run. I'd had it with this new arrangement. I would move out until Katya left, or maybe longer if my "big brother" continued to not see the error of his ways. I took off for the seawall and headed down to Second Beach.

As I neared the pool I saw a crowd of people and I recognized a few faces: Pat, Matt, Danny, Adam, Katya and a whole bunch of others I didn't recognize. Not wanting to be seen, I changed direction and headed for Denman Street where I saw Eddy in front of the Greek restaurant and joined him.

"Why are you here?" I asked. "Shouldn't you be at the beach with the Katya fanclub?"

He just smiled and shook his head no. Eddy is such a cool guy; he knows exactly who he is. He never doubted who he was or what he wanted in his life. I told Eddy my morning events with Ace. He whistled when I had finished, and shook his head to indicate this was a doozy, and finally not all my fault.

We talked about how much trouble I would be in when I returned. The mood Ace was in, he wouldn't be listening to reason. We debated options... running away to a nunnery was at the top of the list. Calling my dad, I thought about that for a bit. Ace could probably have used Dad's help right then just with his own stuff, you know, advice and that sort of thing.

All of these options would make me look like the bad guy. I needed something that would make him sweat and realize the errors of his way. If I played this right, he would be begging me for forgiveness and it would take his mind off Kristine.

"Eddy, I have an idea and all I need you to do is sneak into my house and grab Kristine's number off the fridge. I need to appeal to Kristine's sense of feminine justice."

"Montana, are you sure you want to drag Kristine into this?"

I told him my plan. He gave me an interesting look, one of amusement and grudging respect.

"Montana, I have to give you credit. That is brilliant, but it could go completely wrong. It may be the first place he looks or seeks solace. He may lose it and when he finds you, make sure you won't sit down for a week. If he gets desperate enough, he may call the police and then your dad will be contacted."

That last comment made me pause. I didn't usually think these things out. As everyone knew, I was "the girl charging the hill with the toothbrush." This time would be different. It would go the way I had pictured it, I just knew it would. So, with Eddy on board, he got Kristine's phone number. I called, and part one of the plan fell into place.

Kristine welcomed me with open arms after I told her how mean Ace had been. The fact my clothes were two days old, I hadn't showered and I looked exhausted, helped. Using the Katya situation to plead my case—as Ace, and everyone but Eddy, were suffering from temporary insanity—played right into her own thoughts and feelings.

Kristine took me shopping and to the spa. She provided me with the royal treatment. I had never been to a spa and was in for a real treat. Kristine ordered a massage, haircut, manicure and pedicure. For the first time in forever I felt and looked amazing.

Imagine my surprise when, on day two, Ace showed up at her door, desperate, distraught and in need of feminine support. Damn Eddy, he had been right. I hid in the bedroom and listened to him sob as he related the story to Kristine.

Kristine and I had devised a plan in case this should happen. She knew I was afraid of Ace and what his reaction might be. If this didn't go perfectly, I would be made. She and I had eye contact through the crack in the door. I gave my assent for her to begin the bargaining process with my brother.

"Ace," she began, "I may have an idea of your sister's whereabouts. I'm reluctant to tell you, however, as you seem to have a problem with your temper and I'm concerned for Montana's safety."

"You will tell me everything, Kristine, and you will tell me now!"

I loved it when Ace displayed so perfectly what I had been saying all along. She gave him a stern look and their eyes locked in silent battle.

"Okay, Kristine, I give up. I'll do whatever you ask. I just want my sister back."

"Montana is afraid of you, Ace. If I tell you where she is, you have to promise not to lay a finger on that girl."

"Kristine, no one tells me how to raise my siblings. Are you telling me it's okay for a sixteen-year-old to run away from home and scare the crap out of her family? Is it okay for that same girl to rebel against authority and not be disciplined for it? How would she learn not to do it again? She is being a brat, Kristine and is playing you. She's a smart girl and you're naïve in the ways of Montana."

Damn, my brother was smart. Kristine had grown up in a feminist household. "I am woman, hear me roar" routine. I had played her to an extent, and she was realizing it. In the bedroom, I was starting to fidget and was getting nervous. Think, Montana, what to do now? I came out of the bedroom and stood in front of my brother, ready to play my last hand, the martyr.

"I thought this would be the last place you would look, Ace. I figured I would get a week of peace before you found me. You came here knowing I was here; Eddy must have broken down and told you. You just played the same trump card I did, big brother and used your ex-girlfriend to do it. Congratulations." His expression morphed from relief, anger, and then surprise at my words. I'd totally nailed him and he knew it.

"Kristine, for what it's worth. I had a great time getting to know you better. I'm sorry for the inconvenience I've caused you. I really did think that if anyone could talk some sense into my stubborn brother, it would be you. I was wrong. I should go home now."

Kristine studied us before replying. "Ace, how about I leave for a bit, and you two have a talk? With me gone and no one to interrupt, perhaps you two can come to some arrangement. What do you think?" He agreed, and she left us.

"Montana, is it true what Kristine said? Are you afraid of me?"

"Not exactly, although you can be scary. I wanted you to be scared. I wanted you to think about what had happened. If I had stayed and done what you had said, nothing would have changed. I don't feel it's fair to get punished for things I didn't do, or be forced to do things for others when they should be doing them."

Fortunately, Ace had a cooler head this time around. "Well, Peanut, it seems we have both learned a lesson this time. What do you think I should do about your running away? If the roles were reversed, how would you handle it?"

I hated when he did the role-reversal thing. I like thinking like a brat, not an adult.

"Well," I sighed. "I would ask for your forgiveness for being unreasonable. Then I would tan your hide."

"Good answer," he said, "and for that I'm letting you off the hook. If it happens again, you won't sit for a week, got it?"

We both apologized to each other, and everything was done and over. When Kristine arrived a half-hour later, I was giving Ace a hug, and we were good. We both thanked Kristine for all her help and went home.

Chapter 18

November 1981

Lessons. I wish they all turned out as positively as the one with Ace. No one ever said life was fair, I get it, but at what point could one simply say, Let me off the roller coaster. I'm done?

July 1981

The next morning, I was due at the Masters' new residence to help Ralph unpack. I arrived bright and early and knocked on the door. When Ralph's brother answered, he didn't want to let me in. I pushed past him and walked into Ralph's new room. He was sitting on his bed with Leigh on his lap, and they were deep in a kiss.

They turned their heads and saw me in the doorway. Ralph stood up so quickly that Leigh fell off his lap.

"Ouch," she said as she landed on her ass on the floor.

"That is not all that's going to hurt by the time I'm through with you." I walked over and grabbed her by the hair, yanking her to her feet. I was just about to deck her, when Ralph stepped in and grabbed my arm. He got a hold of my other arm, and then pinned them behind my back. He told Leigh to leave. She swaggered to his door and blew him a kiss and shut the door behind her.

"Let me go," I demanded. "Ralph, how could you, and with her? Yuck! Why would you do something like that with a slut like Leigh? She's done everyone!" I knew my voice was shrill and probably resembled a wailing banshee but I didn't know what was worse, being cheated on by Ralph, or who he cheated with.

"You were right when you said keeping this thing between us would be hard, Montana."

"So now what we had is a thing? What happened to the lovesick paramour who gave me the golden necklace?" Ralph blushed but didn't answer my question.

"Leigh is available and it just sorta happened. It wasn't intentional, I swear. If it's any consolation, being with her is nothing like being with you. You are special, Montana, and our time together was special." He let go of my arms when I began to cry.

"*Merde*," I said, as I headed for the door.

"What does that mean?" Ralph asked.

"It means 'good luck' in French," I answered, and walked away without another word. I felt bleak, no other way to describe it. The sun was shining, kids were happily playing, and yet an emptiness settled inside of me as I bussed it back to the West End. Skipping my stop, I jumped off closer to Chrissie hoping she had time to talk. She was just leaving to go and have breakfast at McDonald's.

I joined her, and while she ate, I drank coffee and relayed everything that had happened since I had last seen her. She sympathized and she told me to look on the bright side.

"It sounds like Katya will be busy at the museum and things can somewhat get back to normal." she speared a piece of pancake but stopped before putting it in her mouth. "I'm sorry about Ralph, that must really sting."

"It was inevitable, but it feels worse than I thought it would. I mean Leigh, like what the hell. He's handsome and talented, so why scrape the bottom of the barrel like that?" I attempted a laugh, but it fell short.

"Maybe he wants someone that is easy and poses no challenges for him. Some guys like that. He's got a new life, maybe this is his do-over. I gotta get going, I have a date. Will you be okay? I can always cancel."

No way in hell would I be a pansy and hold back my bestie from a date. "I'll be fine. Have fun."

"Where is everyone?" I asked Alex, when I arrived home.

"Wreck Beach for the day," he answered.

"Why didn't you go with them?" I asked.

"I got tired of watching Katya treat everyone like her personal slave," he said, with a grin. "Besides, we need to practice."

While we were tuning up and waiting for Otter to show up, I told Alex about Leigh and how it had ended with Ralph. He said he was sorry. I said I was over it.

"Yeah right, Mo. He's the first guy to ever break it off with you. I suspect it will take your ego longer to recover than any feelings you had for Masters."

I rolled my eyes at Alex. It would take a while, but I knew Ralph was right; I had called it back in the school hallway that day when he first approached me. He was leaving us—me and Alex and his life—behind for a new one. I guess he just hadn't been ready to see it then. However, the logic of the situation didn't remove the sting of being dumped any easier. Our relationship would be too hard to maintain with us playing in different bands and living in different places.

We practiced for a few hours and then decided we needed a pierogi break. The three of us headed down to Hunky Bill's for some food. We chatted along the way about our gig the next night. It was a rough crowd, and the location had no air conditioning. I made a note to myself to find a small motorized fan to attach to my drums. It would keep my hair out of my face while I was playing.

Gig night had arrived, and I was nervous. Ralph was gone, and his brother was no longer carting our equipment for us. Alex had struck a deal with Eddy, which worked out perfectly for all of us, as he lived three doors down. We no longer had to do late night unpacking, as Eddy had the key to our house, so he could unload whenever. As long as we had the stuff set up for the next practice.

Eddy had to pull over twice to let me throw up. We arrived early enough to set up and then go outside for some fresh air before the first set. When it was time to begin, I made the mistake of looking out at the crowd. Ace and

Kristine were there. They had reconciled after Ace had found me at her place, and this was their first official date since their reunion. My eyes roamed and caught sight of Adam, Danny and Katya entering the building. Crap! My knees began to shake.

"What is your problem?" Alex whispered.

"Did you see who's in the crowd?" I whispered back.

He nodded.

"Alex, if I screw this up, I will never live it down, and Adam will know without a doubt that I'm an idiot, and you and Otter will never be famous and, oh my God, who am I kidding? I can't play, Alex, this is a mistake."

"Montana, look at me," Alex said.

"I have a message for you from Ralph. He told me to give it to you if you got nervous."

He handed me the note and I quickly read it.

Dear Montana,

I know I'm probably the last person you wish to hear from right now. But I had to let you know how proud I am of you. You have a natural talent, a natural gift. You are easily as good as me, if not better. I thought it would help to let you know that I get the jitters before every gig. It's normal. Don't work the music, Montana, let the music work you, let it flow through you. Remember you are the instrument, and the music is playing you.

Love you lots,

Ralph

That was all the encouragement I needed. I looked at Alex and nodded my head to signal I was ready. I watched for the signal, then closed my eyes and felt our first song;

it came across a bit wooden. I worked on abandoning my thinking and just being. I forgot about the audience and did exactly as Ralph had said.

I lost myself to the rhythm, to the soul of the music.

With the end of the first set, confusion set in, until the applause reminded me where I was. Alex signaled to me, and I followed him off-stage.

"Did you feel it?" he asked breathlessly when we were backstage.

"Of course I did. I always do, it's you that doesn't like it," I replied. "We shared the energy, Alex, and not just you and me, but the three of us. Otter, too. It's like we joined in the middle somewhere and our sound wove together."

He grinned like a little kid. He told me to go outside and get some air while he talked to the crowd forming around the backstage entrance. I stood out back in the alley, letting the success of the last forty-five minutes sink in. I was just getting ready to go inside when Ralph turned the corner and headed toward me.

He gave me a big hug of congratulations as he had caught the last two songs and I thanked him for the encouraging note.

"Montana, you are worth every drumstick you ever threw at me," he said with a grin. "You were fantastic and the three of you together was almost magical."

I gave him a hug and said I needed to go back in for the next set. I watched him walk back down the alley. I had no idea then that it would be the last time I'd see him—alive, that is. When I went inside, I found Otter backstage having a smoke.

He looked up and grinned when he saw it was me.

"Montana, I got to tell ya, I've never felt the music like that before. It's like you and Alex pulled me into some energy vortex or something."

I laughed and shared with him what it had been like for me. Then, Alex was calling us back on stage for our second and last set of the evening. If it was possible, I think the second set went even better than the first. I didn't have to cut everything else out to be present. I could participate and still be present.

Katya came up a few times to dance. I think she was trying to draw attention away from us and to her heart-shaped ass. Normally, that might have worked but tonight was all about us, the band and our first and possibly only performance. Seeing a girl drummer was such a novelty she was ignored and walked off the floor a few times, seething mad.

It was a one night gig so afterward we packed up. Ace and Kristine wanted to take us out to celebrate; I declined, as I was exhausted from the energy surging with the guys, who seemed completely fine. Instead, Ace took Kristine out. Danny stayed and helped Eddy and us pack up.

Every time I looked over at Alex and Otter they were grinning from ear to ear. I smiled faintly at their exuberance. I would get used to it if I continued with them. I wondered what was going to happen next. I was only supposed to play this gig to help them out of a jam. I knew they would want me to continue now that we'd had such a successful night.

Adam left halfway through set two to take Katya out. He would be bringing her back to our place later. Oh good, I thought, I didn't have to see her until tomorrow. When we arrived home, I went right to bed and passed out immediately.

It was in the early morning that I awoke to giggles coming from the living room. I thought Ace had left the television on. I got up to go and turn it off, but when I opened my door, the giggling stopped. I stood, puzzled, but heard nothing else.

Thinking I had just been dreaming, I slipped back into bed. I was almost asleep again, when I heard more giggles.

This time, I got out of bed and turned on the living room light. I rubbed my eyes. "I must have been having a nightmare." Spread out on my living room rug, were Adam and Katya. She was naked and on top of him. He had his pants undone and down a bit. Adam was looking directly at my shocked expression when he began to explain. Katya cut him off before he could say anything coherent.

"Don't worry about her, Adam. She's only a child."

I turned around, turned off the light, and went back to bed. I wished I could have gone back to sleep, but images of them kept haunting me. The next morning, both Adam and Katya were gone. Alex was still in bed, and Ace had gone to work.

I went to the kitchen to make coffee and found Danny already drinking a cup. So, I poured myself some and sat down at the table with him.

"Did you hear anything weird last night?" I asked him.

He said no, but he was blushing when he said it. I decided to leave it alone. After lunch, Otter came over, and the three of us rehearsed some new songs. I was still playing under the premise that I was a temp, yet hoping that Alex would make me part of the band and do the negotiating with Ace.

I wanted it to be me. I wanted to be the one. It was good timing for me with school done and no dance classes. I had nothing else to focus on other than visions of Adam with Katya and Ralph with Leigh. When we broke for the day, we headed down to Bill's again. While we were there, we spotted Chrissie walking with Blair. Alex turned away and focused on his food.

"She still loves you," I said to Alex. He only nodded in response.

We parted ways with Otter, and Alex and I took the long way home. We didn't talk about anything specific, just enjoyed each other's company. When we arrived we found Adam sitting on our front porch.

"Hey, what's up?" Alex asked Adam, as we climbed the steps to the porch.

"Not much," Adam replied, "Just brought Katya back, so she can change before we head out for dinner."

"Oh, how perfect," I said sarcastically. "The pampered princess and the rich boy out together."

Adam looked guilty and asked to speak with me privately for a moment. Alex stepped inside.

"Look, Montana, I feel bad about the other night. I didn't want to be here, but Katya likes everything her way."

"Well, Adam, don't feel so bad. She didn't do it because she feels anything for you; she did it to get back at me for moving the attention from her to the band. What surprises me is that you fell for her crap. I thought you were smarter than that."

I left him on the porch and passed her on my way back in. She said nothing, but nudged me on her way by.

"Alex," I said. "I'm going to the beach for a swim. Wanna come?"

He did, and we found a bunch of our buddies were there, including Eddy, who had a nice supply of rum he shared with Alex and me. We relaxed and just hung out with our buds. We had a great day playing in the water, throwing the Frisbee and drinking rum and Cokes. No pressure, and we both forgot all the burdens from the past weeks and just chilled. We were a little hammered when we arrived home later that evening. Ace and Danny were both home and sitting at the kitchen table when we walked in.

My happy relaxed spirit fled at the expressions on my Ace and Danny's faces. Something was seriously wrong.

"Is it Dad?" I asked, panic freezing the blood in my veins.

"No, but we have something we need to tell you both." Ace patted the chair beside him. "Come and sit with me, Montana."

I wanted to run and not hear what they had to say. I just knew that whatever they were about to say would cause an irrevocable shift. I sat where he indicated but he quickly pulled me onto his lap. My panic instantly escalated to fear. Alex's eyes found mine when he was sidled up close to Danny. He was as scared as I was.

"Earlier tonight," Ace began, "Ralph and Leigh were out on a date. They were jumped on their way home from the movies. Someone had a knife and stabbed Ralph... he died within minutes," Ace finished.

I was in shock. My brain did not, could not, accept what it had just heard. I couldn't breathe. I tried to tell him that he was wrong. We had just seen Ralph. How could he be dead? I was hyperventilating, unable to draw much needed air into my lungs.

"Breathe, Peanut," Ace placed me on the chair and grabbed a paper bag, he held it over my mouth and nose and talked me through breathing. Thankfully it worked but that was only the beginning of my reaction. I alternated between crying and babbling throughout the night until I finally passed out from emotional exhaustion. Ace stayed with me, but I didn't remember any of this myself. Danny told me about it later, much later, when I finally became coherent.

Chapter 19

November 1981

Ralph. A very clear image of him interrupted the movie. His green eyes twinkled. He looked the same as I remembered, but he would, wouldn't he?

"Hello, Montana." His green eyes sparkled with amusement.

"Hey, Ralph, it's been a long time, how are you?"

He didn't answer at first, just gazed at me, through me more like.

"Montana, do you know where you are?"

"Not exactly, but as it's white, my best guess is the hospital. Or, with you here, maybe heaven?"

The Ralph image smiled, kissed my cheek, and disappeared. His parting words floated in my mind. "More to come." More to come? What the hell did that mean? A very unpleasant image took up residence. Ralph, more specifically, what happened to me with his passing. Now we were getting to the beginning of whatever this was. "No. I can't. Ralph, get back here damn it, and take me with you. Please."

I waited but Ralph didn't return. "Alex, just let me go." *Although my request wasn't spoken aloud, just as my calling to Ralph also was all in my head, I was in a coma after all, but I felt Alex reach inside of me somehow. Letting me know he was here with me.*

July 1981

The next morning I awoke with Ace's arms wrapped tightly around me. Opening an eye, I saw that we were in my room and he had his body curled around mine, sound asleep. Last night's news played in a loop and as it did I began to cry. Once the tears started, they didn't stop.

Ace did his best to console me but three days later, I still couldn't get past it. I didn't see Alex during this time. Danny was busy helping Alex cope with his own grief and loss. Ralph had been his best friend since they had been six years old.

Ace tried to feed me, but every time I would throw up. Day four was the funeral, and it was so bright outside and very warm. Ace helped me get dressed as I was as weak as a newborn kitten. He gave me some water and soup before we were to leave and I threw up everything.

A sad looking group of pasty individuals climbed into Eddy's car and drove to the funeral. Ace and Danny looked about ten years older and I swore I saw a gray hair on Ace's head. Alex was so thin he looked haggard. I saw all of this but was completely detached. The lights were on but nobody was home.

There was a large crowd at the funeral home when we arrived. Ralph and his family had been well-liked and it showed in the turnout. Again I observed all this but remained analytical, stuck in my brain the way I had at mom's funeral. People spoke with Alex and me, including his parents. I had nothing to say. I just watched the sea of faces swim before me.

When we were given a moment, Alex and I headed up to Ralph's casket. He looked impossibly young, too young to be in there. I could feel Alex beside me and instinctively grabbed his hand. We gazed into a face that had always been a part of our lives.

Silently, we spoke to Ralph, our words meeting and running into one voice. We told him how much we would miss him, how much we loved him. I had brought along a pair of drumsticks, ones he had used to teach me how to play.

I laid them on his chest when I leaned in to kiss him goodbye. Alex leaned in and kissed him also. That's where thought ended. I found out later that Alex and I had not wanted to leave. In fact, we would not leave the coffin.

Ace and Danny had to drag us out of there. On the way home, I threw up in the car and then passed out. My brothers could not wake me, so they took me to the hospital. I was told that I teetered in and out of consciousness for several days.

When I came to, I saw a familiar hump on the chair next to me.

I had major déjà vu. I had been here before, or maybe that's where I am. I tried to speak to Ace, the familiar hump, but had no voice. I tried again, and the sound I made came out as a whisper. I tried again and my voice came out sounding croaky, but loud enough for my brother to hear me.

"Montana, thank God," he said, "I didn't think you were going to make it. How are you feeling, Peanut?" he asked as he rose from his chair.

"Hungry," I croaked.

He laughed, and I gave him a typical Montana grin, a lopsided one side grin. He said he needed to go and phone Dan and Alex to let them know I was awake and to find the doctor. After a brief look-over by the doc, and a broth delivery by the nurse, the guys showed up. I was being spoon-fed my broth by Ace, when Alex and Danny strolled in.

"Okay, now that you are all here," I said, sitting up in my bed, "would one of you care to tell me what's going on and what I'm doing here?"

They looked at each other, all wearing expressions of mild confusion.

"While you're at it," I continued. "Perhaps you can tell me why Alex looks like a stick, and you two," I said, pointing at Ace and Danny, "look so damn old?"

"You think I look like a stick," Alex retorted. "You should see yourself."

I croaked out a laugh.

"Montana," Danny said, "Do you remember the funeral?"

I thought for a moment. I let images flash, and I saw a car ride, and a funeral parlor. I saw a casket, and I could have looked over the edge to see who was inside, but my mind recoiled from it.

"No".

Ace and Danny excused themselves and left me and Alex alone together in the hospital room. We said nothing but studied each other silently. I could feel him reaching out tentative thoughts to me. I could have reciprocated but chose not to, and shut off the communication.

He looked like he was going to say something when Ace, Danny and the doctor entered the room. The doctor checked my vital signs and looked into my eyes for a while before he spoke.

"Montana, do you know why you're here?" he asked.

"Not really. Ace said I passed out in the car, so he brought me here."

"Montana, you were brought in for severe dehydration and malnutrition. You had been to a funeral earlier that day with your brothers and your friend Eddy. Do you remember that?" he asked.

I shook my head no. He smiled down at me and then exited the room with Ace and Danny. A while later, the trio came back into the room, along with a woman I hadn't met yet.

"Montana, I'm going to let you go home later today. But only if you follow the stipulations I'm going to lay out for you, do you understand?"

I nodded.

"No rebellion, Montana. Your brother Ace has told me how strong willed you can be. This time, however, that type of behavior won't work. If you don't do as I say, you will be back here, and it will be for a while. Do you understand, young lady?"

I nodded again, and he went over the list of stipulations. One of which was to come to the hospital weekly for counseling visits with Dr. Treakle who he introduced to me as my therapist. Whatever, I thought; I just wanted to go home. I would agree to flying to the moon if I could get away from the four plain white walls and hospital bed.

Later on that day, that's exactly what I did. Ace carried me from the car to my bed, and I promptly fell asleep. When I woke up, Ace brought me toast and apple juice. I made the conscious effort to chew while he chatted about nothing in particular.

"Dad will be home in a week, and he can't wait to see you," he added with a smile.

"Dad," I said, puzzled. "But, I thought you were my dad."

It was his turn to be puzzled. He grabbed a frame from my bookcase and held it up.

"This is Dad, Montana. Don't you remember him?"

I shook my head no. He stood and cleared away my dishes.

"I'll be back in a moment, Peanut," he mumbled absently.

When he came back, he had a photo album in hand. He opened it up and showed me pictures. There were pictures of a young Ace with a football in his hands, then Ace a little older on Halloween and dressed as Spiderman. Ace again, this time in a football uniform, and beside him stood a woman who looked like Danny and me. Must be an aunt, I mused.

There were photos of Alex and me in matching jumpers with the same woman. There was another of her with Ace... I'd have to ask him who she was. Alex entered my room just as he was closing the album. I asked him who the woman was in the photos.

"Are you serious?" he asked with an incredulous look. "That's our mother, you twit."

"Our mother? Where is she? What did you do?" I turned my glare on Ace. "Have you been cheating on her with Kristine this whole time?"

Alex left the room wearing a look of alarm. Danny came in next. He sat on the edge of the bed and asked me questions.

"Montana, what is your last name?"

"Stanford, dur." He smiled.

"Montana, how old are you?" he asked next.

"I'm eight," I answered.

"Okay, Montana, I think it's time for you to have a nap, I'll check on you in a bit."

I lay on my bed feeling like I was afloat in my body. Nothing seemed real. I could hear the guys in the living room talking, and I thought I heard Ace sobbing that he couldn't take anymore. I didn't know what he was referring to.

I drifted off to sleep. I call it sleep, but it was more like a daze. I imagined it would be like this for a vampire; you're not dead, not alive. When I woke, Dr. Treakle was in my bedroom.

"Hello, Montana."

"Hello, Dr. Treakle."

"How are you feeling?"

"Okay I guess, why are you here?"

"I have something I want to show you, Montana."

Ace scooped me up and carried me to the garage and set me down on my feet.

"I heard you can play the drums. I was wondering if you would play for me."

"Me? I don't know how, but I can try."

I sat down on the stool and picked up the sticks. As soon as I held them in my grip, a flood of memories engulfed me, starting with placing a set of sticks in a coffin and continuing at lightning speed and ending so abruptly I gasped at the physical impact, almost toppling off the stool. With tears streaming down my cheeks, I played for what seemed like hours, until exhaustion won, and I dropped my sticks. I looked at the expectant faces.

"I understand now, it was Ralph in that coffin." I struggled to my feet. I took in Ace's exhaustion and my heart broke open. I wobbled to my brother and placed a hand over his heart. "Thanks for being so awesome, Ace, you are an amazing man, and the best brother a brat like me could ever have."

He grinned as he scooped me up. I was asleep before we got halfway across the garage. Next time I woke up, I was aware of two things, one, the sun was shining and the birds were singing, and two, I felt better. Well enough to stagger to the kitchen in search of the rest of the family.

My brothers were drinking coffee and deep in conversation, which ended when I entered. The guys asked me how I was feeling. When I said better, they asked me if I would like to see Ralph's grave. I didn't, but felt I should.

The four of us headed out and stopped on the way to buy flowers. It had been just over a week since Ralph's death. Already it felt like so long ago, only because so much seemed to have changed. Change brought on an illusion of the passage of time for me. Sometimes I asked myself if I was the same girl I was a week ago.

It was a beautiful sunny day, and although our task was sad, our spirits were up. We stood by the grave, the four of us, silent in our own thoughts. I was the last to stand and leave. I put the flowers and a set of drumsticks on the grave. As I put the sticks down, I heard his laughter.

An image appeared of him chasing me after I had hidden his sticks. I grinned, inspite of the sadness I felt. It was when we were pulling up to our house that I remembered Katya. I hadn't seen her since I got home and wondered what had happened to her.

"Hey, Danny, what happened with your friend Katya?" I asked.

"I don't think Katya is used to dealing with trauma, Montana. When we received the news of Ralph's death, she had Adam come and pick her up and take her to a hotel downtown."

"Oh," I said. "I thought perhaps she would have moved in with Adam, being as they were, um, getting on so well with each other."

"No way. The way he told it, after he picked her up, she started complaining about you so he offered to drop her off at any hotel of her choice, and as far as I know, that's the last time he saw her."

Good for him. He was restored to his unique position of stud in my I-want-to-be-with-this guy book. Ace attempted to send me to bed a few minutes later. I said I was fine and tired of being tired. I wanted to sit on the couch for a bit and have some soup. So, he brought me soup, which I love, and orange juice, which I hate.

God! How long was this compromising-for-the-good going to take? I missed being me, I thought with a lopsided grin, running wild and free.

"What are you grinning about, Mo? I know that grin, and it has trouble written all over it."

I laughed, and assured Ace I was just sifting through some memories that were making me smile.

"When is Dad due home?"

"Day after tomorrow. Now drink your juice and if you eat all your soup, I may give you a treat later," he said, in a teasing tone.

"Yes, sir." I saluted, "and maybe if you guys stop babying me, we could get this house cleaned up. It's a mess. You guys are real pigs when I'm not around keeping you in line," I said, with a grin.

He was about to say more when there was a knock on the front door. It was Adam. He asked me if I wanted to go for a walk. I said I wasn't up for it, but I could manage to go for a drive. So, with threats of violence against me and Adam if I didn't drink an entire bottle of water and a small orange juice on the drive, Adam and I set off.

I hadn't been in his car since Alex and I went with him to pick up Danny from the airport.

Gosh, how long has it been? Three or four months? It felt like forever ago. He told me he had asked to see me on several occasions but I had been an off-limit zone. Instead, he had kept tabs on my progress by telephone with Danny.

I didn't know how to respond to that and said nothing. We drove up to the lookout point on the top of Cypress Bowl. "The view of the city from here is so beautiful."

"That's not all that's beautiful." Adam replied.

My face went beet red. How could he say that when I looked like a scarecrow?

"Montana, I have something for you," he said, handing me a large envelope. Inside was a drawing of Ralph, Alex and me. It was remarkable and very detailed. He even had a set of drumsticks in Ralph's hand.

"Adam, it's beautiful. Thank you so much."

He reached forward and kissed my hand. We did not speak, just looked at each other. It reminded me of the first time I had met him. A short time ago, yet it seemed a lifetime. I began to fidget not knowing where to go from here.

"I brought my camera. Would you like to take some pictures?"

"I'll watch while I drink my mandatory OJ." I rolled my eyes. Adam laughed and stepped out of the car. I watched and asked questions. He'd show me what settings he used to capture the different angles and lighting. When I finished my juice he handed me the camera. Between the two of us, we shot around a hundred pictures. Good thing he could afford the film and developing costs.

Adam said he had a darkroom and would show me how to develop the pictures. I was excited and asked him not to develop these ones without me. I had taken some of him and I wanted to be the first to see them.

"Adam," I said. "Do you remember that night you drove me home from the movies?"

He nodded, a smile forming on his face. Brat, he knew exactly what I was going to say. "I have a confession. I looked at that notebook you had sitting between our seats and read the poem."

"I know. I wanted you to."

My eyes widened with surprise. "You did? But why?"

"Montana, I also have a confession. I knew you were at the theatre that night, and I sat down a few rows away and watched your facial expressions as you watched the movie. You were so absorbed in it you didn't notice me. Later, I purposely placed my notebook on the seat so you would read it in the hopes that I would give you a ride home."

This was a surprise. Adam came across, relaxed and chill, yet behind his calm demeanor lurked the mind of a tactician.

"Everything I've done has been intentional." he continued. "Honestly, Montana, I've known about you for a long time. Danny has always spoken of his talented family, but always raves about his beautiful sister. I fell in love with you just from Dan's descriptions. You're tough and strong, yet you're also vulnerable. My heart and soul are drawn to you. Montana, you were born to be with me; you're my muse."

My jaw was scraping the bottom of the car. I studied his face, making sure this wasn't a joke. I leaned toward him and wrapped my arms around his neck. His lips caught mine, he licked the seam of my lips and my body felt like it was on fire. We were literally on top of the world but I was higher than that, floating on cloud nine.

What had felt impossible was happening. This was real and he was finally mine.

Chapter 20

November 1981

He would be my one regret, Adam. I knew deep in my heart he and I were end-game, or would have been if things had turned out differently.

August 1981

Ace wanted some alone time with Dad and went by himself to pick him up from the airport. Danny, Alex and myself took that time to put finishing touches on the house. We'd really let it get filthy during my illness and of course, taking care of me and working full time had kept Ace and Danny too busy to worry about the house.

We watched out the window and when Dad and Ace pulled up we were out the door in a flash and launching ourselves at Dad. "Look at you two, thin as train rails you are. I almost can't tell who is who."

I punched him playfully in the arm. "Hey, I'm offended." I grouched, but it was all in good fun. Nothing that man could say would offend me.

"My goal this trip is to fatten you two up." Dad laughed. I loved the way his eyes crinkled when he was in a good mood. Ace had that same crinkle but I rarely ever saw it. Right now his expression was one of pure relief. With Dad here, Ace could relax and be himself instead of having to play caregiver.

"Tonight," he said, while pulling us all in for a hug, "the sky's the limit. Where do you want to go for dinner?"

"Well Dad, that's nice of you, but how about we do that tomorrow night? Danny, Alex and I have been cooking up something special for you."

"Even better," he said. "I've been dying for a home-cooked meal."

We entered the house and Dad made some comments on how clean it was. We sat down in the living room and lost ourselves in the stories Dad regaled us with, stories of working on the rigs, and sea life he saved along the way.

Every few minutes, one of us would disappear to the kitchen to make sure the food wasn't burning. Other than that, we sat riveted by his tales. I swear, that man had done enough living for three people.

When dinner was ready, Alex and I served and the five of us sat down to a wonderful meal. By the time dinner was done, I was exhausted. Being with Dad had driven my meager energy stores into overdrive and I felt completely depleted. Dad noticed and asked me if I was okay.

"Yeah, Dad, I'm fine. Just a long day for me. I think I'll go lie down. Why don't you guys go out and have fun?"

"Good idea, Peanut, let's go, guys."

Ace hesitated. It would be the first time I had been alone. I could tell that he wasn't sure if he could trust me. I gave the big lug a hug and told him I was fine.

"Honestly, Ace, I am so tired," I swayed as I spoke, "I am just going to sleep, but if you're truly worried," I said, with a wicked grin, "Adam could come and babysit."

"Oh, very funny, ha, ha," he said, as he picked me up and then deposited me on my bed. He turned on my lamp, got me some water and headed out. I lay in bed, staring at the ceiling and feeling the soothing quietness of the house. I never realized how loud my brothers were, especially when they were all home.

I rolled over to play a tape that Adam had made for me. He called it yoga music; I called it sleepy-time music. Still, it soothed my restless spirit so I listened and picked up my journal. I'd always wanted to have a journaling habit, but like most things my writing had been inconsistent, until Dr. Treakle. She made writing my feelings mandatory as part of my recovery.

Next thing I remember was Dad turning my light off late in the night. I woke up the next morning and found a note from Dad on the kitchen table.

Peanut,

Dan and I are out golfing, and Ace is at work.

Rest up. I'm taking everyone out tonight.

Love, Dad.

There was another note, this one from Ace. It was a reminder of when and what to eat and a message to call Adam.

"Who needs a mother, when Ace is around, eh sis?" Alex joked. He joined me at the table and told me about their night while we waited for Otter to arrive for practice. This was the first since Ralph's death. I felt I was ready and also really needed to get back some strength in my arms.

Alex and I had just finished a late breakfast when Otter showed up. I quickly went to call Adam but had missed him, so I left a message to say I was in the garage with the guys if he wanted to stop by.

We started off with some easy stuff and stepped it up, once we were warmed up. When we took a break a bit later, Ace called. Alex answered and immediately started mimicking Ace. Otter and I were howling with laughter, Alex was dead-on with his impersonation. He repeated, "How's Montana doing?" Just like him and then pretended to stick his finger up his nose before answering deadpan.

"What a pain," he said when he hung up the phone. "Mo, remind me to never get sick or injured. I don't think I could handle being mothered by him."

We went back to rehearsing, but Otter called a halt a short time later.

"Alex, are you okay?" he asked. "I mean, you're playing perfectly, but your energy is missing."

I had noticed also, but thought it was me and my lack of the usual energy. I was waiting to see if our music melding was going to kick in before I brought it up with the other two.

"I'm feeling disconnected," he sighed. "I've been feeling disconnected from you, Montana. When you reverted to your younger self, I lost my connection with you. It was very disconcerting, I take that back. It was downright scary. I never realized how tied we are. I never noticed because it has never been taken away before."

He was right, of course. It was the missing ingredient in our playing. Without our connection, Otter had nothing to ground him. As a result, we were all playing perfectly, but woodenly. I had to trust the process, and let go.

"You're right. We need to reconnect for this to work. How about we play the last song we played at our last gig? Imperfections and all, let's play until the music plays us."

The guys agreed, and about halfway through the third time playing, the connection kicked in. Then we just let it rip. Alex led us through a medley, and we played our hearts out. At some point, Dad and Danny entered the garage. but we didn't notice until we finished and they clapped.

It was the first time Dad had heard me play, and I was deeply invested in his feedback.

"That was something. I'm very impressed with how well you all play, individually, but together, it's quite magical." Then a glint of mischievousness entered his eyes. "I don't know, boys, but I think the girl might have outplayed you both." His comment caused us all to laugh. He sent me a wink and I gave him a huge smile in return.

"Otter, why don't you join the family for dinner tonight, we're going to that steak house, Stuart Anderson's, that's close to your house." Dad licked his lips and Otter readily accepted. We dispersed to get cleaned up and I snagged the only shower in our house, first.

I opened the bathroom door when I was done to see Adam standing with a bag in each hand.

"Your dad invited me," he said in a way of explanation. "I did some shopping on my way over and bought you something. I hope you like it."

The label on the bags read La Chateau, so yeah I was pretty sure I was going to love whatever was inside. I took a minute to appraise his appearance. He was dressed like a prep, in a pair of white loose fitting cargo's. The bottoms were rolled to the ankle bone and he had on navy loafers and his shirt was white which accented his tanned skin, and a slung over his shoulder was a navy jacket. His look was simple, sexy, and hugged in all the right places.

I was still wrapped in a towel, but grabbed the bags, delivering a quick kiss to his cheek as I did, and hightailed into my room. In the first bag, wrapped in layers of tissue, was a white mini skirt. I slid it over my hips and it hugged what little curves I had. Next item was a matching halter top in white and a navy shawl. He was dressing us to match. My eyes fluttered at the image of how we'd look together.

In the second bag were navy heeled sandals with ankle ribbons and a cute leather evening purse to finish off the look.

I opened the door and peeked my head out. "This is so amazing! Thank you so much."

"Let me see," He insisted. I opened the door fully.

"Damn, woman, you look even better than I imagined. Can I do your hair and make up?" I was floored. I had never had a man so much as cut my hair, never mind an updo for a date. Being an artist, though, I was sure he had definite ideas as to what to do with my heavy brown mop, so I said yes. He had me sit at my desk in front of my make-up mirror, and brushed my long locks into submission, then swept it up into a loose bun. He loosened a few tendrils and curled them around his finger, they bounced down and framed my face perfectly. How the hell did he know to do that? Adam dug through my assortment of makeup. He applied a bit of feather light foundation, mascara, a little liner for definition around the eyes and soft, pale pink lipstick, like a frost that shimmered in the light.

I gazed at my reflection in wonder. I'd never looked so good, yet he'd kept it so simple. I was impressed. "Adam, I don't know what to say. You truly are an artist if you can take a girl like me and make me look hot."

He laughed. "Montana, you were born hot, you just didn't know it. I'm just showing you how I see you."

I took another look in the mirror. "Well, if this is how you see me, Adam, it's no wonder you wanted to date me. Hell, I'd want to date me." When Adam and I came out of my bedroom, we looked like a Hollywood power couple. The guys were sitting on the couch waiting for us. As soon as the rest of the Stanford men saw us their mouths dropped.

Except Dad's, he wore a wistful expression. "Well, boys, we won't have to worry about your sister tonight. It's quite clear who she belongs to."

Alex smirked, knowing this was exactly what I'd alway wanted to be, with Adam, as a couple. Still a blush crept up my neck and spread across my cheeks. Thankfully, no one commented.

Adam and I drove in his car, and Dad and the guys went in Ace's car that Dad gave him when he'd left to work on the rigs. Otter lived super close to the restaurant and met us at the entrance. He did a double-take when he saw me but didn't say a word.

Adam set his hand on my lower back, guiding me as the hostess brought us to our table. It was an oddly intimate sensation. I mean obviously I didn't need help getting to the table, but his hand on my back was comforting all the same. Dad noticed and nodded his head in approval.

We were laughing so hard, we thought for sure we'd be kicked out. Especially when Otter told the ostrich story, even though we'd heard it before, Dad hadn't, and almost fell off his chair. After dinner, we headed up Raspberry's. It was not licensed for alcohol, so under-agers could go in. The guys had played here before, and we all knew the owner.

He greeted us when we walked in and said some words of condolence regarding Ralph. He also let us know that it was jam night and anyone could go up on stage and play. Otter suggested that we add ourselves to the list. Ace didn't think I should, as I had already played today and I needed to be careful about not expending too much energy. I said I was fine but I couldn't play in a miniskirt anyway, and to stop fussing. Ace gave me *the look* and I sat closer to Dad. It was quite humorous actually. I stuck my tongue out at Ace. He didn't notice, but Adam did. We shared our first private joke. You couldn't count that time at the beach with the booze because it wasn't a joke and Alex had been with me.

Adam handed me another bag.

"Another gift. You are full of surprises tonight, Mr. Northrop."

Adam smirked. "I thought you might need a wardrobe change. Besides, you never wear heels and even though those are only two inches, I bet your feet are already killing you."

He wasn't wrong. I tugged out more tissue paper and wrapped inside was a pair of white leather pants and a pair of navy tennis shoes with a cute bow on the toe bed.

"Really, Adam?" I said, "Is there anything else hiding I should know about?"

"Maybe, Mo, but if there is, I'm not telling you what or where."

Another blush stole over my face and I excused myself to change. I examined my ass in the bathroom mirror. If anything, the pants revealed more than the mini, not less. I rejoined them to have their jaws drop all over again. Alex had put in our names, and we were up after the next set. Everyone got to play two songs. So after the current song finished the next band came on for two songs and then us.

We played our two songs, the applause got us two more songs and then one finale. We kept the energy high and the dance floor full. When we were done, the next band brought the pace down a bit and Adam took me up for a slow dance.

I had a hell of a time letting him lead, and kept stepping on his feet.

Dad also took me out for a spin on the floor. He was really good. He told me he and my mom used to enter dance contests together. I was intrigued and wanted to ask him questions, but the tempo changed, and Dad wanted to take a break.

I was wiped and asked if I could go home. Dad cut in saying we had a busy day at the Pacific National Exhibit, known as the PNE, tomorrow and we should all get some rest. Dad and the guys left and drove Otter home. I went with Adam in his car. We were the first to arrive.

"You were incredible tonight Mo."

"That's because I knew you were watching me and it gave me all kinds of tingles."

"Oh? So you're telling me that you get hot and bothered when I watch you strut your stuff?"

"Very." I unclipped my seat belt and slid closer to Adam. He angled his head and claimed my lips, probing the seam until I opened for him. A low growl came from his chest. I gripped his hair and tugged him closer wishing to feel him as deeply as possible. If I could climb inside him and take up residence for the rest of my life I'd die a happy woman one day.

As the heat between us became frenzied, light shone in the interior of Adam's car. I groaned as I pulled away. Adam exited the car and came around to open my door. He gave me a light kiss on the cheek before saying goodnight to my family. I watched as he pulled away and waved until he was out of sight.

"He's a good man. He'll take good care of you one day."

I hadn't realized that Dad was standing behind me. "I think I'm perfectly capable of taking care of myself, don't you?" As soon as the words left my mouth I regretted it. How stupid of me, hadn't everything up until this moment proven that I wasn't capable? "Scratch that."

Dad chuckled. "Sweetheart. You have been through a lot, and everyone needs someone now and then."

I leaned into him for a hug. "Thanks Dad. I needed to hear that."

I went inside and stripped out of my sexy new clothes and carefully hung them up before passing out on my bed.

Chapter 21

November 1981

In some ways that night marked a transition in my life. Adam was no longer a secret, or considered out of my reach. He'd taken the next step for the both of us, when he'd taken me to Cyprus Bowl and admitted his feelings.

August 1981

The next morning, Dad and Danny were up first, fixing breakfast and making coffee. I sat down to have my morning juice and watched the activity.

"Dad," I said. "Do you mind if we invite Ace's girlfriend to attend the PNE with us?"

"Ace has a girlfriend?" he asked with amusement, edging his words.

"Yeah. Didn't he tell you about Kristine?" I looked at Danny. He was shaking his head. "You mean they didn't reunite after that Katya fiasco, after all." I mumbled, "I thought when he brought her out to the club to see us play that they were officially back together."

I gave a brief explanation and brought Dad up to speed on their relationship since last fall leaving out anything that may incriminate me.

"She sounds lovely. I wonder why he never brought her up?"

"They broke up, Dad," Danny cut in, "but Mo is right. Ace and Kris were pretty hot and heavy until Katya arrived. I should have never insisted she stay here but I had no idea what type of person she really was. In New York she was this cool chick with a hot accent and we had fun."

Dad patted Danny on the shoulder. "Maybe you did him a favor, son, if they fell apart so easily maybe she isn't the right one for Ace."

I was offended, for Kristine. After all, she had been amazing to me since day one. "That's really unfair. Kristine is amazing and Ace is totally in love with her, he's just so damn stubborn. I wonder where he gets it from." I lifted an eyebrow at my dad.

He chuckled and nodded his head sagely as he pointed at himself. "If you can make it happen, Peanut, go for it. I would love to meet her."

Dan rolled his eyes at me but didn't say a word. I checked on Ace. His room was empty and the shower was on. Perfect, he wouldn't overhear me. I quickly dialed her phone number.

"Hello?"

"Kristine, it's Mo, our dad is in town and I would really like for you to meet him. We're going to the PNE today, and I want you to be there. You and Ace are perfect for each other. You're both just too stubborn to admit it."

"Montana, does your brother know you're calling me?"

"Does it matter?" She remained silent. "Okay fine. No, he doesn't but you two need to make up."

"You are such a meddler."

"I know, but that's why you love me. Oh, and wear something sexy, something to drive him crazy." I hung up the phone before she could say no and rubbed my hands together.

Adam swung by and picked up Danny and me. I was about to get into the front when Danny called shotgun.

"Seriously, dude? Don't you think your sister, *my girlfriend*, should ride shotgun?"

Danny grumbled something about being loyal to a brotherhood, causing Adam to laugh outright. But he still climbed in the back and I gave Adam a brilliant smile of approval.

Dad, Ace and Alex stopped by to pick up Otter on the way, and met us. Once inside we made our way to the log ride. Adam and I took the front. Dad and Alex took the back and the four of us got drenched, but we didn't care because it was a hot day and we knew our clothes would dry quickly.

At the shooting arcade we saw a bunch of kids from school including Chrissie and Kim. We talked for a bit before heading to the roller coaster. I checked my watch and saw it was time to make our way toward the Ferris Wheel where Kristine was to meet us.

Our group, minus Dad and Ace, were first to arrive. They'd gone to check out the livestock. In the distance I could see them making their way toward us from the east. From the west, Kristine was also making her way toward us. I rubbed my hands in anticipation of their reunion and hoped Ace wouldn't blow a gasket. At the four-way, the crowd passed and Kristine and Ace almost bumped into each other. We were close enough to hear her gasp in surprise. Then she wrapped her arms around his neck, no easy feat for her tiny stature, and tugged him down for a kiss.

Smart woman, action instead of words was sometimes the best way. I silently rooted for her to win my brother back. Ace tugged Kristine tight against his body and deepened the kiss. I couldn't hold back a huge grin.

"I take it this was your doing?" Adam wrapped an arm around my shoulders.

"Yeah and it looks like it worked."

"I'm not so sure."

Ace released Kris and introduced her to Dad, then his gaze found me and his eyes hardened. "You may be right Adam, but he'll thank me, eventually, I'm sure of it." The three of them joined us and we made plans to disperse and meet up later. Ace didn't say a word to me but his body language said he had plenty to say. I'd worry about him later. Right now I wanted on that Ferris wheel for alone time with Adam.

As soon as we had lifted off he wrapped an arm around my waist and slid me right next to his side.

"That's better. You're right where you belong." His words did all kinds of crazy to me. My heart hammered in my chest, and the constant blush I experienced around this man was present. Our kisses were hot and my body grew even hotter right along with them. I pressed myself against his muscular frame, needing more from him.

"Montana," he said, coming up for air. "I know how you're feeling, I'm feeling the same way, believe me, but this isn't the time or the place."

"Then take me to your place, I don't want to wait any longer. Please." It felt horrible to beg but I needed him.

"No, Montana, we need to wait," he said, with a look of resignation in his eyes.

I was growing impatient and frustrated.

"Wait for what, exactly? I don't think I can. I'm about to go out of my mind and I don't even understand it, I've never had this before," I said, pulling back from him.

"This is called hormones and sexual urges—and love, I hope," he answered, with a small smile.

Love, so this is love. Yes, I loved him, I had really, since reading that poem in his car that first night I met him. Yes, this is love, my heart had wings and I could fly, to quote Cinderella. "Adam, you know me better than just about anyone. Look into my eyes and tell me what I'm thinking right now."

He did, he looked, then he looked right through me. I was naked, completely exposed but I didn't look away, I didn't hide. I allowed my soul to be seen. Alex knew my soul, of course, as we were born with the twin connection. It was not by choice, but I could also shut him out when I chose.

This was the reverse. I chose to stay still and let him roam through my soul, my spirit. My heart shuddered for a moment as I felt his energy take hold and then cradle it. He peered into me and saw himself peering back.

He broke our connection and closed his eyes for a moment. I followed suit but probably for a different reason. His probing made me feel different, and loved in a way that was completely new, and with my eyes closed at the top of the Ferris Wheel I really did feel like my heart had wings.

"I love you, Montana, heart, spirit, and soul, now and forever."

My eyes opened to see him gazing at me in a way no one ever had before.

"I love you too, Adam. I love you with every part of my being, but I guess you know that already?" He grinned and took my hand and placed it on his heart. I closed my eyes and felt the regular *thump,thump*, and then I felt more, I felt its compassion and love and hope. I saw images of his dreams, I felt his heart rate change as I cast deeper.

I roamed his heart like alien terrain, picked up his emotions one by one and lovingly placed them back. I could feel this blue-purple aura all around us, pulsing with our combined life force. At that moment I felt a seal press us irrevocably together.

When I opened my eyes, Adam was crying. Not hard, desperate tears, just a few gentle tears that came from the deep sharing of our bond. The ride came to a stop and as we pulled away from each other the distance I had mourned when we parted before wasn't there. I still felt the full force of our connection even though we were no longer touching.

Hours later, I found Dad at home, alone. I made us some tea and flopped down on the couch. He told me Mom stories and had me laughing so hard I almost peed myself. The man must have been a bard in a past life, his storytelling was unparalleled.

Then we discussed Danny's birthday. I suggested throwing a backyard party with all his family and friends. The band could play. Dad could take Dan golfing, which would take several hours, and the rest of us could get everything set up. He thought the plan was great.

"I should get some sleep. I'm exhausted."

"Before you do, Peanut, I have something for you. How about you get ready and I'll go dig it out."

Just as I climbed in bed Dad knocked on my door. He held a box in his hands. "This was your mothers. She told me to give it to you when the time was right. I feel that time has arrived." He kissed me on the top of my head and quietly left the room, closing the door behind him.

I slowly opened the lid. Inside was a few books and a smaller box. Pulling out the books, included were her diary and her cookbook, that she always had out when I was little. She used to tell me and Alex during our tea parties when she moved from eastern Canada to the west, she'd met an array of interesting people that shared recipes with her. She'd compiled them into a book. I ran my hand over the familiar images, loving the feel of the worn cover.

I set the box aside, wanting to take a look at the diary.

The date started with her in grade seven. I found her writing style amusing; she'd had a good sense of humor. I flipped through the pages, reading about her thoughts on boys and her first crush. I flipped to her last entry. Where she writes about having to leave her babies. Poor Mom. her words drip with the sadness she felt. I felt unsure about reading her most intimate thoughts and closed the diary. I had plenty of time to read through and for the first time in my life I was in no rush.

Chapter 22

November 1981

Mom's box held more treasures than I realized at the time. Her words brought comfort, and her stories made me laugh, and sometimes made me cry. It was bittersweet and so were my dogged memories of her. I really missed her.

August 1981

Alex and I discussed how best to set up the band in the backyard for Danny's birthday. Two days wasn't a lot of time, but with help, I knew we could make it happen. Finally, it was decided, to do it right, we needed a platform, and called Eddy to come over.

Alex showed him what we had in mind and he said he and Pat would get on it and have it done for the morning of, and get our equipment set up. They also volunteered to go and get the booze; we were getting some kegs. That was three pressing items we could check off the list.

Otter's mom ran a small catering company so we hired her to do all the food. Ace and Alex would pick it all up, as well as the ice and coolers that we were renting. Adam would stay and help me decorate and do the final touches.

The best part of setting up a secret birthday bash was keeping Danny completely in the dark. We let him think that the family breakfast at Smitty's Pancake House was his idea. When in reality, it fit in perfectly with Dad's surprise gift and throwing him off the thought of there being anything further happening that day.

Dad called in a favour with an old friend to deliver Dan's gift to the restaurant. To keep Danny in the dark, we purposely had him sit with his back to the bank of windows that faced the front with Ace, Alex and I facing the window. Just as we were finishing our meal, the three of us witnessed the gift arriving. The man driving it, the dealer I supposed, jumped out and expertly placed a huge red bow on the front. It was hard to keep a neutral expression, but Dad had Danny so engaged in a golfing story that he thankfully wasn't paying attention to me.

Ace stood up and stretched, "Hey guys, check this out." Danny turned and gazed at where Ace was pointing. "Check out that cool car. I guess someone is getting a gift."

Our group stood transfixed as who we assumed was the car dealer came into the restaurant and walked toward our table and handed Dan the keys.

"Happy Birthday, Dan the Man," it read on the key chain. The car dealer, whose name was Joe, shook Dan's hand and gave him his business card, and wished him a happy birthday. Danny just stood there, mouth opening and closing with nothing coming out. He looked like a guppy.

"I don't know what to say. Are you sure? I mean, how, this is so much, too much," Dan finally said to us, but his gaze was focused on Dad.

"Dan, you are a good kid, a talented kid, and you have a bright future ahead of you. I'm proud of you son, we all are. I got a bonus this year, so this car is a gift to you. You deserve it."

Dan gave dad a huge hug, tears quickly forming in the corners of his eyes. "Thanks, Dad. It's the most amazing gift ever."

"Enough teary stuff," Dad said. "What a soft crew I have here. "Part two, Dan. We're heading to UBC to play some golf. Meet you all later for dinner."

The two of them left in Dan's new car. Ace and Alex left in Dad's old car and I headed for home to meet up with Adam. I had an hour and stopped along the way to grab a few items. Outside the bakery I felt someone watching me. The hairs on the back on my neck stood and adrenaline flooded my system.

Gazing around I noticed a group standing in front of the community centre. Scanning the faces, I picked out Nick and Mercy. Her eyes bore into me with an evil gaze.

There was no other way to describe it, her energy was negative and hateful. No one in her group noticed her vibrating with hate as she glared at me, or me gazing back impassively, not giving away any of my power to the she-devil.

She noticed my control—hell, I noticed my control, as it was not something I'd had before. Must have been Adam's positive influence as that was the only thing different in my life. Maybe the band? I didn't remember having this power before Adam and I began dating.

I continued on my way and arrived home just as Adam pulled up. I helped him unpack the decorations, and told him about Danny's car and his face when he saw it, the walk home, and seeing Mercy and her group.

Mercy hadn't come up in discussion for a long time. He reminded me of that beach party night when he had caught her staring at me and had noticed how she looked at me.

"I know that Eddy, did, or said something to have them leave you alone, but don't count on that lasting forever. He told me she and her "posse" joined a Chinatown gang. Their initiations almost always include permanent bodily harm. They usually end up killing their victims and usually by stabbing."

I mulled that over, but refused to harp on it as that would ruin my day. Instead I focused on the set up for the backyard party. Our theme was Hawaiian, complete with a tiki bar set up in the empty pond, so anyone sitting at the bar could feel like they were drinking in a pool. Well kinda, sorta.

We hung up the patio lights, set up the tiki bar, leaving plenty of space for the kegs of beer. As we finished with the puka shell votive candle centrepieces, Alex and Ace showed up with the beer, coolers and food.

Eddy and Pat finished putting together the temporary stage and the set up of our equipment. Adam completed the look by pinning a hibiscus floral garland along the front of the stage.

The six of us stood back and examined our handiwork. It looked amazing, we were transported to Hawaii. Well, we took Adam's word for it as none of us had been to Hawaii.

With everything set and an hour to go before the big surprise, I went in the house for a shower and a beer. Hot summer day, I was sweating for hours, just needed to freshen up and chill out. Between the back door and the bathroom, I downed a beer. I burped freely in the shower. Drying off and getting dressed I downed another and then Adam came in my room with a beer for us both.

Good man, I reached for him and the beer, leaning in for a deep kiss. God, he smelled good, and looked good too. Always the Greek god, sexy perfection, regardless of what he wore. His lips incited a riot of emotions in me, but as I leaned in hard for more. He pulled back.

"Montana, how many beers have you had?"

"This is my first one, and thank you for bringing it to me."

He gave me a wolfish grin. "You are not going to start lying to me so soon in our relationship, are you?" he asked, one brow rising in question. "Because if you are, I guess I'll have to punish you by not taking you out on the amazing date I had planned for later tonight."

"Third! This my third," I confessed, a coy grin spreading across my pink cheeks.

"I see my girl is inspired to be good when she's given a reason. Noted."

He gripped my hair, holding my head in place, while he kissed me with the heat I was craving.

"And when you're done with that third beer, you won't have any more until you have three glasses of water." He was so nonchalant, that for probably the first time in my life, it didn't bother me that someone, him, was telling me what to do.

"Well, of course," I answered, batting my eyes innocently. He laughed and pushed me down on my bed. He held my wrists above my head. My body bucked trying to gain friction as he peppered kisses down the column of my neck.

"I'm being very serious." He drew his head back and held my gaze. "I need a healthy you, so we can continue to have fun and move forward. Okay?"

"Yeah, yeah, Ace number two, I'll drink the water." I was joking, not joking. I didn't like what I felt was negative attention, not unless I was the one creating it myself.

His sensual lips drew into a line before he spoke. "I want you desperately. Not so I can be in charge of you or because I feel the need to control you. It's only because I want you, who you are. Do you understand?"

"Yes. You're saying that we need to be on the same page and you're helping me to get and stay there so we can have fun."

"Exactly right. Now where was I?" He nuzzled my neck. Goosebumps erupted on my skin and a little moan escaped my lips. This man drove me crazy with a need I could barely comprehend.

"Adam, why did you pick out my outfit, and dress me, and do my makeup the other night?" It had felt so special, but I couldn't help wondering if there was something more behind the gesture.

"Because I want to take care of you and show you that I am capable of noticing and attending to your needs as a boyfriend, but also, I wanted to highlight your beauty, and that you're finally mine."

He released my pinned wrists and rolled onto his back and tucked me into his side. I snuggled in with a heart rending smile. I felt his struggle and snuggled closer to him. Our breath fell into a natural rhythm and any stress I'd been feeling vanished. I closed my eyes and must have fallen asleep. The slamming of the side gate alerted me to the arrival of our guests.

Eddy watched out for Dan's new car and when they parked out front, we all quieted down.

From the front of the house, everything looked completely normal. I could hear Dad saying he couldn't find the house key, and that they should go through the back, as someone surely left the screen door unlocked.

"Surprise!" We yelled when Danny came through the gate. Poor guy, we scared the crap out of him. He must have jumped three feet in the air. Then he was laughing and being clapped on the back and hugged.

Someone handed Dad and Danny a beer, and the party ramped up a notch. "This looks incredible," Dad exclaimed as he took up residence in one of the lawn chairs.

"I don't know what to say." Danny added. "Breakfast and the car were enough of a shock, but a party too? It's a lot."

"Don't say anything." Adam wrapped an arm around Dan, "just enjoy it." The two of them went out front to take a look at Danny's new car. I grabbed myself a beer and headed up to the Hawaiian platform to play.

Alex and Otter had both grabbed a few beers to keep their whistle wet during our set. We played for about two hours when I'd decided I'd had enough and needed a change of pace.

After a full day and a few too many beers, I stepped away to get ready for my date with Adam. I downed a few glasses of water and instantly felt better, and a much needed shower washed away the sweat from playing drums in the summer heat.

Back in my bedroom I found a bag on my bed. I opened it, and inside was a slinky black cocktail dress with matching ballerina flats and a pair of heels.

Adam's eyes twinkled. "Start with the heels, but change to the flats when your feet get sore, duh." He rolled his eyes, copying me perfectly. I broke out into peals of laughter.

He took me out to dinner, a very high-end restaurant that I had never heard of, Papillote. I had no idea what that meant, so I asked Adam. He grinned, "It means 'In Parchment.' It's the English translation for the name of the restaurant, which is French. Originally, their signature dishes were wrapped in a sort of pastry that looked like little gifts. It's a style you find in a lot of French and Italian cooking."

He talked about the different types of game meats he had tried at the restaurant including moose and quail. Yuck! He said one day he would take me to Africa, so I could eat some wild game there. *Hmmph*, I didn't know if that was my thing.

If I went to Africa, all I would want to do is ride on an elephant.

Looking over the menu, I chose what any true Canadian would, a good old-fashioned steak from a locally sourced ranch. Adam ordered something in French. When it came, I asked what it was. He said it was better if I didn't know. I was fine with that. We had a bottle of amazing wine. They didn't ID me, which was way cool, so I drank alcohol at a restaurant for the first time.

When dinner was done, Adam asked me what I wanted to do next.

"I want to see your house," I replied.

"No problem," he answered. "I only live ten minutes away."

True to his word, ten minutes later we pulled to a stop in front of a huge gated entry. Adam entered a code and the gates swung open. The curved driveway led upto a mansion with a circular driveway.

He didn't park out front however, but in front of a separate entry way that led over the five car garage. "I don't live in the main home anymore, but in my own apartment."

"That's cool." For once I was at a loss for words. I was surrounded by wealth and in comparison, our backyard party felt tacky. My life felt tacky when compared with the opulence in front of me.

"There is a gallery that attaches my place to the house that I use when I'm here." Adam parked and opened my door, taking my hand to help me out of his vehicle.

"Your father must be very successful." Dan's words from months ago about our differences echoed. Maybe my brother had been right all along. Maybe Adam and I didn't fit, despite how we felt about each other.

"He is." Adam unlocked the door and escorted me up the wide staircase. "We weren't rich when we came here from England. My dad worked really hard as a labourer before creating his mega-enterprise.

At the spacious landing, he unlocked another door that opened to his place. He continued to chat about his dad and the early days while uncorking a bottle of wine, leaving me to look around.

The main area had an open floor plan. The kitchen, dining and living areas were one generous space. Most of the furniture was modern, and the appliances were stainless steel. I had never seen stainless steel appliances before. The only space not perfectly organized and clean was the dining area which was set up as his art studio. The kitchen had a long island with hand-carved stools from Thailand perched on one side. I had never seen this type of setup before, and admired it. He had an interesting assortment of modern and antique pieces spread throughout the rest of the living space.

I wandered over to his work area to take a look. Having never been to his house, I'd only seen his work in his sketchbook and was excited to see more. He had an unfinished sculpture under a blanket, and the walls that were solid were decorated in his art. All perfectly framed and hung. With wine in hand, I surveyed the art, and Adam did brief explanations on each of his pieces.

I noticed that as I followed the walls down the hall from the kitchen toward the separate rooms, there was a distinct shift in his work. The stuff in the living and dining areas were cold, almost a calculated perfection. However, as I followed the work down the hall it shifted, not necessarily the content, but how it was represented.

"Adam, is the art out there newer or older than these?" I indicated the hallway walls.

"Older, when I moved into this space from the main house a few years ago, I started decorating the main spaces first. Why do you ask?"

I took a deep sip of the rich deep ruby red wine in my glass loving how the flavors burst on my tongue. "I'm noticing a shift in your work the farther toward the back end of the house we go. Why is that?"

"My earlier work lacked a muse. Since I've gotten one it has impacted my work—for the better, I'd say."

"Oh," I answered. "So, Katya must have loved seeing your place. She must have noticed the difference in your work. Was she happy to know that she was your muse?"

I remembered her perfection; she must be the one, I thought.

"Montana, you're too funny. My earlier work reminds me of Katya, icy perfection. She is not, nor has ever been, my muse. You are my muse, and you have been for awhile."

"But I have only known you for what, a year maybe? How could I have been your muse back in" I peered at the framed piece that said 1980 on the plaque - "1980? What is a while anyway?"

"Follow me," is all he said. He led me to the last door on the right and flipped on the lightswitch. I stood in wonderment, speechless. Every inch of wall space in his room was covered in drawings of me: standing, walking, cheerleading, playing drums and things I could never imagine. Horseback riding, standing on a yacht with my hair blowing in the breeze, on a mountain top. Echoes of my image again and again.

He couldn't have done all of these since we started dating, or even since we met... there were hundreds. His voice broke through my thoughts.

"The early ones that are less detailed are from Dan's descriptions of you from before we met. I went to a few basketball games and other events that Dan told me you would attend, just so I could get a look at you. Many of my first attempts at a more realistic impression came from watching you from the stands. The rest are after the night we met and I drove you home."

I was still speechless. Looking around, I felt that Adam had everything. Wealth, a family that loved him, talent, but it was sterile without me. I really saw at that moment that our financial backdrops had nothing to do with him as an artist. That Adam needed me and that thought made me uncomfortable. I couldn't remember a time being needed by anyone. If anything, I was alway the one in need. It was an odd feeling for the roles to be reversed.

"You have a spirit like a ray of sunshine, Montana, and for some reason I'm able to capture it. You also have a dark, fathomless spirit, and you are powerful. I capture that also. You have altered my art, made it better, because I've learned to see the spirit and heart of that which I paint. That's why you are my muse. Before you, it was elusive, I couldn't capture the essence of a thing, only its perfection. You have opened up a power within me to see on an energetic level, instead of with just my eyes."

"Kinda like what Alex, Otter and I share when we play. They didn't have that with Ralph, but for some reason they do with me. All this time I'd thought it was the twin connection but maybe it's more than that."

He reached out and tugged me in for a kiss. When he pulled away, his eyes burned with an intense heat. "I have waited a long time to paint you in the flesh, Montana. Would you pose for me?"

Chapter 23

November 1981

I never said anything to Adam about all those things Katya had said, but they had swirled in my mind as he set the scene to draw me.

August 1981

"You know I will." I sounded way more confident than I felt. I don't know why I was nervous when the man had enough drawings of me to fill three galleries, but I'd been unaware of them. This was deliberate and I was here, wide open with all my flaws on display.

He guided me to a stool, and placed water and my wine within reach. Adam seemed intent on his work, too intent like he was striving for that perfection seen in his earlier work. I had no intention of being a subject. If he wanted to be inspired by his muse being in person, then that's what I was going to give him.

I removed my shirt when Adam's eyes strayed from me to the paper. When he looked up his eyes grew wide. His jaw dropped but words seemed to be eluding him. Sidebar, yes a new word from Mr. Webster.

I was beginning to think I'd made a mistake, until he grabbed a few sheets of paper and fresh charcoal. Without a word, he started drawing at lightning speed. He called these preliminary sketches that he would use later for paintings.

A few minutes later, I took it a step further by removing my bra. I gulped with nervousness remembering what Katya had said about my body when she'd scrutinized me in front of all Danny's art friends.

The next time he looked up his eyes nearly popped out of his head. I tried not to laugh as his hand picked up the pace. Without missing a beat, he grabbed another sheet of drawing paper and continued to draw furiously.

I needed to pee, so he worked on some details while I went to the bathroom.

I looked in the mirror, I mean really looked at myself and tried to see what he saw. My eyes were a brilliant blue but cloudy with doubt. I didn't used to look like that. All the crap from this past year had taken its toll on me. Somehow I'd missed the changes in my eyes.

Then an idea, and the sassy sparkle I was used to seeing returned. "Now that's what I'm talking about. You go girlfriend."

I returned without jeans, wearing only my sexiest pair of undies, and instead of sitting on the barstool, I laid myself out on his couch. His green, cat eyes drank in the sight of me and another fervour of activity took place. Finally, I rose and put my clothes back on and he rolled over onto the floor, exhausted, sweat glistening on his smooth tanned skin. I joined him on the floor and cuddled up into the crook of his arm.

"Adam, I want to stay here with you tonight, right here curled up in your arms."

He grinned and pulled me into a tighter grip.

"I want you to stay, too. What would Ace say if you called and asked him?"

I got up and walked over to the phone.

"Let's find out," I said with a laugh.

When I heard his voice on the phone, I asked to talk to Kristine. He hesitated, but passed her the phone.

"Kris," I said, "I need a favour. I'm at Adam's, and I want to stay the night. We won't *do* anything. Would you talk to Ace for me?"

She said she would call me back. When the phone rang, I picked it up expecting to hear her friendly voice. Instead, I heard Ace.

"Montana Margaret Stanford." I winced. I didn't like it when Ace used my middle name. It was my mother's name, and I hated that hearing it meant I was in deep shit.

"Yes?" I said in a small voice.

"Please pass the phone to Adam. I would like to speak with him right now!"

I passed the phone to Adam and mouthed that I was sorry.

"Yes-sure-okay-you bet... no problem, Ace," he said with a laugh. "No need to worry. If she doesn't do as she's told, I'll find a way to make her obedient."

I heard Ace laughing as Adam hung up the phone. "What did he say?" I asked anxiously.

"He said that you shouldn't have been so gutless and should have asked him yourself. He also said that if you didn't do as you were told to thrash you," he said, the last part with a big nasty grin on his face. I blushed a deep crimson as an image came to mind.

"Montana, I'm curious, why did you ask Ace and not your dad?"

"That's an easy one, my Dad was well on his way to being hammered when we left, so most likely he is passed out by now. Ace, though slightly sloshed, would have been the responsible one. And, let's not forget my brother's fragile ego. If I hadn't asked him, he would have pouted."

Adam laughed. I loved the way his eyes would shine and the corners crinkle.

"Now about that thrashing—"

"Yes, you'd better be a good girl." He laughed.

"—You know he was only kidding," I finished.

"Maybe," Adam answered. His eyes glittered with mischief, "but just to be on the safe side, you'd better follow my orders," he said, trying not to laugh.

I decided to play along. I sauntered up to him and wrapped my arms around his neck and pulled him in for a kiss. I pressed and rubbed against him, driving us both into a frenzy of desire.

"Someone has to say no, Montana. I guess it will be me." He pulled away then and led me down to the bathroom where he had an extra toothbrush ready for me. We brushed our teeth together, which was weird. I mean, sure, sharing the bathroom I'd done plenty of times with Alex, but we were twins, womb mates. Having the hottest guy ever brushing his teeth beside me was surreal. He grabbed me a t-shirt to wear and we climbed into bed. I was asleep as soon as my head hit the pillow.

Chapter 24

November 1981

My first night with Adam would be ear marked in my mind like a passage from my favorite book. I'd wanted him so badly, to lose my virginity. To be taken and for a moment, be immersed in him, mind, body and soul. Being naked and pressed against him had been so enticing. I had felt alive in a way I had never experienced. I would regret dying a virgin, not having been with Adam in that way.

August 1981

The next morning, I woke to the sound of whistling and the smells of food cooking. I lay in bed, letting last night wash over me. My gaze ran over the abundance of drawings until one in particular grabbed my attention.

It must have been done after I had been beaten up. He must have come to the hospital to see me when I was unconscious; I know he saw me a few days later when he brought a gift from Danny. This drawing was different; I would swear that was the hospital bed.

In the drawing I was awake. He'd minimized the cuts and bruises so they were not the focus. It was the eyes that held me rooted to the spot. The pain they expressed was powerful.

The drawing was not distinct; it was more ethereal in nature and done with so much emotion it brought tears to my eyes. Grabbing a tissue from the side table I quickly wiped my tears and was about to get out of bed, my grumbling tummy wanting to follow the delicious smells wafting to me when he yelled out to stay put.

A few minutes later Adam came in bearing a silver tray with flowers, and laden with plates of breakfast food, coffee and orange juice. Good God, I thought yet again, who is this guy? It was a strong reminder of the wealth he belonged to, a much different world than my own.

The reminder of his wealth was like an iron fist in my gut, and instead of eating what he placed in front of me, I began to fidget. I grabbed my coffee mug and faced the opposite wall which was filled with me and suddenly everything was just too much.

"Montana, why are you so fidgety? Don't you want what I made?"

I was about to reply, nothing at all was up, when he said, "and don't bother saying nothing. You're a bad liar."

This actually made me smile. He was this perfect open book with no issues or hangups. Why would someone like him want to be with someone like me? But instead of asking, I said, "it's your wealth, Adam. I feel so uncomfortable and I don't think I belong with you in your world."

"Montana, listen. I don't need this stuff." He swung his arm expansively indicating his worldly treasures. "If it makes you feel any better, I'll move into the slum and live with orange crates for furniture."

He meant it to be funny, but all I heard was I lived in the slum. "You mean like me?"

"Oh come on, it's not as if you live in the slum, and you know it. Sure your family doesn't have the same material wealth, but you guys own your own home and it's filled with an amazing, talented family. Please don't make us about comparisons, because if you do that then I guess I'd be the one to bow out."

He had to be joking. What did he lack that I had? "How do you figure that?"

"Do you need me in your life? Examine the dynamic here, Mo. If we didn't happen, the guys would be vying for your attention and eventually you'd give into one of them and go about your merry way. If the roles were reversed, and in the same situation, I'd be devastated and probably give up art."

Panic seared me. "What? Why? Please Adam, I don't understand."

"I have been in love with you for a very long time, Montana. You are my muse, and the woman I love. That doesn't happen very often in life and the women that would come after me if you weren't here would only do it for my fortune. My life would be empty without you in it."

His confession was more than I bargained for and the differences between us suddenly appeared to me as a good thing. Maybe we did stand a chance at being together forever.

Letting go of my negative thoughts, my stomach took that as a hint that it was time to eat and growled loudly. I laughed and then dug into the best breakfast I'd ever eaten.

"You're a good cook," I said through a mouthful of omelette.

"I'm jealous of that fork," he replied, his eyes all glittery with an unspoken need.

My cheeks flamed with the innuendo. I didn't reply, what could I say? When breakfast was done, I offered to clean up and do the dishes. He told me to leave them, that the maid came in and did those things. I rolled my eyes at him and said, "Yes, your grace."

He gave me a long look but didn't share what he was thinking.

"Hey, can we develop our camera roll from our day at Cypress Bowl? I really want to see them."

"Sure, get dressed and I'll show you how." I put on my jeans and one of Adam's t-shirts, and the ballet flats he had bought me. He took me down a set of stairs to a room in the garage. It was huge and photos hung on lines across the ceiling.

"That's where we hang them to dry once they've been processed in the developer solution." He answered my question before I could ask. "The process of developing what you saw through a lens, into a tiny negative, and then onto paper was super cool, like magic."

"Oh, I'm taking these ones home. Your handsome face can stare back at me when I'm missing you."

Adam chuckled. "Why don't we go take some more and let these dry. I can bring them by tomorrow."

I agreed and took a drive up to Cypress Bowl, stopping on the way for some bottled Evian to keep me hydrated. We parked at the lookout point. Adam opened the trunk and pulled a plain black box out, handing it to me. I gazed at it quizzically.

"Just open it."

I did and found a camera inside, almost identical to Adam's, but newer.

"This is for me?"

He nodded. "I like giving you gifts and you have talent. Besides, you hog mine when we take photos, I had to do something to reclaim what's mine."

The way he said what's mine sent a little shiver up my spine. "Thank you Adam, this is a lot, but I promise to honour this new gift and take amazing photos."

"You better." he growled. Oh lord love a duck, I was practically panting with that sexy growl. What was wrong with me? Besides the obvious I mean. Like I get it, I should be bowled over by my super sexy Mr. Growly, and I was, but also, whatever was happening between us felt like melding. The more we became a couple the less "me" and the less "he" there was.

It was late in the afternoon when Adam brought me home. Dad was parked in his favorite chair and asked if we'd had a good time. I showed him my camera and told him about the photos we developed. "It was so cool, Dad, I can't wait to show you them. Adam said he'd drop them off tomorrow."

"Speaking of, I'm leaving in two days, and I have some things I want to go over with you and your brothers. Adam, you are more than welcome to stay for dinner and the discussion as well."

That surprised me. Why would Dad want Adam to stay for a private family discussion? Adam didn't seem surprised however and said he'd love to stay. Danny was on dinner patrol, so Adam and I sat down with Dad and filled us in on how the party ended. Then we filled him in on our evening after we left, leaving out the part when I modeled almost completely naked.

Adam assured him that nothing happened between us. Dad just smiled and said he didn't doubt us for a minute. When dinner was ready, the six of us sat down to eat. I was surprised to see Dad had placed a bottle of beer at each place setting, as neither Alex nor I had ever been offered a drink before. I could tell Ace wanted to say something but he held his tongue.

We discussed what needed returning from Dan's party and who was going to do it. Our equipment was back in the garage but the platform needed to be dismantled and stored and the serving trays needed to go back to Otter's mom and the coolers returned to the rental.

As both Ace and Danny were working the next day, Adam and I offered to take it all back. Well, Adam offered, and I said I would help him. The mood seemed to shift a little then and I guess I wasn't the only one who anticipated what Dad wanted to discuss.

Thankfully, Dad got down to the family business talk pretty quickly. "Listen up, Ace and I spent the day with my lawyers and accountants. I'm fifty-eight years old, and I'm not getting any younger."

That had our attention. The room was so silent you could hear a pin drop.

"I have investments, some I started when your mother and I first got together," he continued. "I also have a very good insurance policy as I work one of the most dangerous jobs on the planet. If something should ever happen to me, the four of you will be well looked after. That is after the government gets their share, there should still be about two million in the estate."

I sucked in my breath. Two million—how he hell had he managed to do that?

"Also, I have fifty thousand set aside for each of you, strictly for your own purposes. To use for school, or a wedding—he looked at Adam and me when he said this—or buying a home of your own, or whatever you wish."

I felt a blush creep up my neck to my cheeks and dropped my eyes.

"Alex and Montana, yours will be kept in trust until you're eighteen years old. Ace, Danny, the two of you have access to yours now. One other item. Alex and Montana, if something should happen to me before you become adults, Ace and Dan will be your official guardians. I think, considering what they have had to deal with, they've done an amazing job. They have worked, gone to school and been a continual support to the two of you," he said to me and Alex. "By choosing them both, if something should happen to either of them, guardianship moves to the next brother."

Well, that was some major food for thought. Ace and Danny went over details with Dad and asked questions. Adam listened to their conversation. He grasped what my brothers were struggling to understand and actually helped Dad by translating the more difficult terms into layman's terms.

Without saying a word to each other, Alex and I got up and started clearing the dishes. I washed and he dried, remaining silent while the other four continued to talk .I could feel his mixed emotions about what Dad had shared, and I knew he could feel mine.

I couldn't help but wonder if this strange feeling I had in the pit of my stomach was some weird foreshadowing. I had learned that literary term this past year at school. I was glad to have learned it, too, because I now had a word to describe something I often felt.

Two days later, the Stanford clan piled into two cars and headed out to the airport. I went in Danny's new Mustang. Alex went with Dad and Ace in his car.

I wanted to spend time alone with Danny as our relationship had been changing since his bestie and I became a couple. Some changes were good, like being included and being treated more as an equal than his little sister. Some bad, like resentment for the very same things.

Despite my best efforts to discuss real issues, he wasn't saying a word to me. He was distracted, and probably still processing all that Dad had shared with us at dinner the other night.

I rode with Ace and Alex on the way home. With only a few days left of summer break, it was time to get ready for the school year. Clothes that had fit me a few months ago were baggy and all my pants but the ones Adam had bought me were too short. Alex had the same problem. He had really sprouted this summer.

We planned a shopping day with Danny and Adam, who were in the market for new art supplies, and Kristine who had been promising me a shopping trip and was finally making good on her promise, and of course where Kristine went, so did Ace.

Adam and Kris came from the same environment, the entitled kids, and had run in similar crowds back in high school, and were the same age. It was kinda cool that they were connected; it helped to close our little circle and tie it with a tidy bow. Kris, true to her word, bought me a new look. I was going into grade eleven looking like a superstar.

Adam and Dan spent a small fortune at the Opus art store on Granville Island. Ace was conservative in his style and purchases and Alex was anything but. He got more adventurous in his style and it suited his darker, quiet personality. It would fuel the mysterious persona that his fans already loved about him.

After a long successful shopping day we grabbed Chinese takeout for six and took it to the house. We all got on well and fit together with no struggles. It seemed to ease the tension between Danny and Adam and me.

After cleanup, Adam and I decided to lay on the loungers in the back yard and stare at the stars. I had brought out pillows and blankets, so we could fall asleep if we wanted. Adam was an astronomy buff. He pointed out constellations. We saw a falling star and he called it the "Montana Star."

I laughed and hit him with my pillow. I told him when I found a falling star I would call it the "Adam Heavenly Body" because he was so friggin' gorgeous. He laughed. We held hands and slid into a comfortable silence. Each lost in our own thoughts, I squeezed his hand as I was nodding off.

"Adam... I love you."

"I love you too, Montana," he said, squeezing my hand back.

"I'm going to be fanciful now and I would like you fully engaged in fulfilling my fantasies."

I felt him grin in response but he agreed. "Adam, are you going to marry me?"

"Yes, Montana, I am going to marry you."

This was fun. "Adam, will we have a white church wedding and then live in a house with a white picket fence?"

"No, Montana."

That got my attention. "No, why not? You're breaking your agreement to fulfill my fantasies."

"Well, Montana, that isn't your fantasy."

It wasn't? Well, now I was confused, "Okay, Adam, please enlighten me as to my fantasy regarding our wedding and where we will live."

"As to the latter, there are almost no houses in the West End and as you will want to stay close to your family, you will want a beautiful, opulent penthouse that is decorated to your tastes with a second bedroom, so when one of your brothers is loaded, they can spend the night."

He was going into way more detail than I expected and his logic made perfect sense.

"There will be a work studio in the back of the penthouse to capture the afternoon light, where I can work and still be close to you. We will divide our time between our fabulous penthouse and our family weekend home, location yet to be determined. How am I doing so far?"

He had nailed me, but I didn't want to admit it. So instead of speaking, I squeezed his hand.

"You will divide your time between being with me and touring with your band. You, Otter and Alex will become a huge success and sign with a record label. I will keep you in line and make sure you stay healthy and you will be my muse, feeding my creative prowess for our lifetime together."

Holy crap balls! How was he able to see things so clearly that looked like a muddled mess to me?

"Because of our mutual wealth and success we will have homes all over the world and eventually own a castle in Scotland, which is your dream."

I could barely breathe. The images played as he spoke of them and I could see it all. The life he spoke of, I could see it and I both wanted and was terrified at the same time.

"Adam, is that you fulfilling my fantasies, or what you see as well?"

"I told you, Montana, now that you are finally mine, you will be mine forever. You can count on what I said and much, much more."

I smiled a sleepy smile as I drifted off and wondered if life could get any better.

Chapter 25

November 1981

Experience has taught me that when things are good, disaster is often right around the corner.

September 1981

The new school year began all too quickly. It seemed weird with no Ralph. This time last year, life had been so different for me. This year, life was full already with drumming on top of dancing and cheerleading. Alex, Otter and I had grown closer as a band and as friends.

    The three of us were tight but we needed to be. Alex was so popular, he had a gang of kids from all grades constantly following him around. I don't know how he could stand it. With Ralph gone and Otter being the only other male in the band, his popularity had grown over the summer.

It was interesting to see that, in the short time I had been playing, I had also developed a following. Chrissie, who had been my best friend since grade one, suddenly was too busy to hang out. Her and Kim were with an entirely new crew this year. Deep down, I knew it was the groupie thing for Chrissie. She'd never liked it and hadn't accepted it with Alex, so why would she with me? And Kim? We hadn't been tight since her and Otter broke up.

Otter seemed to be enjoying the new level of attention he was getting as a single bass player of Behind Blue Eyes. Alex was the star, of course, and girls followed him everywhere. Not just girls, but wanna-be musicians wanted advice. He handled all the attention as he always did with ease.

Unlike my fellow band members, I was uncomfortable and was either ducking behind walls or running for a hiding spot whenever I saw fans headed my way.

We were only a few weeks into school when there was a knock on the front door.

Alex and I were home from school and just getting ready to rehearse. I opened the door to find two officers standing on our porch. They asked if Ace was home. I said no, wondering who was in trouble. He asked when he would be.

I shrugged. "Later," I said. "Maybe six."

Alex and I went out to the garage and rehearsed. Otter joined us a little later. The officers at the door were forgotten. When we had wrapped up for the day and Otter had gone, I remembered the officers and told Alex about it.

We couldn't think of anything we had done so we dropped the topic as not applicable to us.

Ace and Danny arrived home shortly before dinner was ready. As soon as the front door was shut there was a knock. Wow, you had to give those cops credit for persistence. As Ace answered the door, a thought occurred to me that those cops had been out front the whole time. They had never left, but why?

That gave me the creeps and a chilly feeling came over me, giving me goosebumps. Something was wrong. The officers spoke with Ace outside. The three of us sat in the kitchen speculating on what all this could be about.

They were outside a good long time when Ace walked in. He collapsed on a chair at the table, and not only was he as white as a sheet, he was trembling. Oh God, I thought, something had happened to Dad, or maybe Kristine?

"Ace," Danny said, sitting near to him and gently grabbing his arm.

"Is there something you need to share with us?"

When he didn't respond, Danny told Alex to pour a large shot of whiskey and bring it to him. Danny made Ace drink it. Then told him to spill it. Ace lifted his head. His eyes were almost empty, unseeing as he shared the news.

"It's Dad," he finally whispered. "There was an explosion. Everyone who was on the rig is dead."

There was a stunned silence. We were too shocked to say a word. I watched Danny's face, saw him struggling to process what we had just heard. I felt very calm, as though I was drifting, an observer of myself, not a participant in my life. I knew this feeling and knew the potential danger but ignored the signs.

I got up from my seat and went to my room to call Eddy and Adam.

Dispassionately, I broke the news and said the guys needed support. I couldn't feel anything, every act and feeling was wooden at best. I shut off, disassociated, while remaining completely aware of everything that was happening.

Eddy was at the house in two minutes and assessed the situation. He called Dr. Treakle who said she'd send a specialist over named Dr. Kelso. Danny seemed to be having the hardest struggle so, after making his call, Eddy took Danny to his room and stayed with him.

When Adam arrived, he came straight for me. He hugged me close and I returned the hug but with no feeling in it. Apparently even my love fled. He looked into my eyes, puzzled, searching for the truth of where I was at.

Before he could fully grasp that Montana wasn't home, Eddy came out to talk to him. Adam disappeared into Dan's room and Eddy went over to Ace and Alex to keep them calm until Dr. Kelso arrived. I didn't know what to do. The Montana on the inside was crying in anguish; the Montana on the outside decided to make tea.

The doc arrived. She took one look at Ace and said he needed to go to the hospital. She said Ace was in a conscious coma and it was similar to when patients experienced brain damage. They could hear everything but could not communicate, giving the illusion of being in a coma, while appearing awake.

His particular version was like acute PTSD, the only way his mind could comprehend the trauma. His condition was similar to my retreating to a different age after Ralph's death. I heard all of this and asked questions about the ways to handle it.

Danny was crying, but she said that was healthy. To grieve so quickly meant that Dan would likely be okay in a few days. Eddy and his parents were going to keep Alex with them for a while. As he was also expressing his anguish in a healthy manner the doc figured, like Dan, he would be okay in a few days and we could deal with the aftermath of counseling when they were ready.

Those two just needed some space to grieve and someone there to take care of them. Eddy's parents had been good friends with our parents and would take any of us in at any time if need be, just as my parents would have done for Eddy.

In the role of best friend, Adam elected to be with Dan for as long as it took. I was going with Ace to the hospital. Someone needed to be there for him and hold down the fort and that someone was me. The doc had tried to persuade me to stay with Dan and Adam but I flatly refused.

I was needed for a change and I was not about to bow down from my responsibilities. Montana and her mourning would have to wait. I locked the door on her and threw away the key. When things were settled with the others, then I could mourn.

Chapter 26

November 1981

I'd known then that my reaction set me on a course of self destruction. I knew but chose not to let anyone else in on it until it was too late. I felt gut-wrenching pain, enough to make my body flinch, an outer sign of my internal turmoil.

Poor Ace. My heart bled for him. In denial and his mind unable to process or accept Dad's death. I totally understood where he was and the fact we were having a role reversal situation.

Dad. I could see his smiling face; it seemed so real as if he was right in front of me.

Smiling down at me and stroking my hair, like he did when I was little and sick in bed.

"Dad, what happened? Tell me about the rig and what happened to you."

"Montana, what are you doing here, darling, what happened to you?"

"I don't know, Dad, all I know is there is too much pain and I want to let go. I want to be with you and Mom."

"Sweetheart, your time will come one day, and soon you will come to the end of the story you're watching and have to make a decision. When you're done here I want you to choose life. Do you hear me? What happened on the rig was an accident and all those men and women lost their lives right along with me. I didn't feel any pain, I promise. Now, let me tell you what I see for you. A long healthy life. You will marry and have children of your own and you will become wealthy in your own right. I promise sweet girl, if you choose to live, all these things will come to pass."

October 1981

I stayed with Ace for five days. He was drugged for the most part. When he was awake he was violent. His reactions were physical. At one point he bolted upright in his bed. I tried calming him down but it was no use. He flailed his arms like a wild man, knocking over his lamp and hitting me in the process, several times. Then he grabbed me. Thank God, a nurse came in time to save me from the chokehold Ace had me in. During his delirium, he mumbled about all sorts of things from his past. Many must have been long before I could remember as I didn't recognize the names he was saying.

The nurse managed to give him a shot and he calmed down in seconds. I had a nice shiner on my right eye, some swelling and a host of bruises but nothing major. Then Ace started mumbling about me in a conversation with Dad. I couldn't make out all of it but it sounded like, "'Dad, what do I do with Montana? She's always in trouble at school. I know she's young, but I can't control her. She's a crazy kid. You'll never believe what she did today after she and Alex watched Peter Pan.'"

On the inside, trapped me, laughed. On the outside, wooden me, just listened. Ace's voice shifted until he sounded like Dad. "'Montana is an amazing little girl. One day she will be your best friend. She will be brilliant and do amazing things with her life if she is just given the chance. She has a spirit that will not be denied, and she will accomplish what most only dream of. You can't control her, Ace, just love her where she's at. Be her brother, not her parent. She already has—had—those. She just needs to be loved and understood.'"

An incoherent stream was all I was able to pick up after that and I think I must have fallen asleep because I don't remember anything else until much later when Adam came by to check on Ace's progress and to update Dr. Treakle on Alex and Danny.

He tried to talk to me, comfort me, but I couldn't feel. His words were empty, bouncing off my hard exterior. It was on day four that Ace came out of his coma state. I was dozing off in the chair by his bed when I heard his voice.

"Peanut, where am I?" Ace mumbled as he tried to sit up in bed, which of course he couldn't, as he was restrained.

"You're at the hospital. You had a bit of a breakdown. If you're okay, I'll get the nurse to take off your restraints."

He looked down at his arms and realized why he couldn't sit up.

"What did I do?"

"It's not what you did, Ace, it's what we were afraid you might do to yourself. You were in a conscious coma, and Dr. Kelso thought it best to drug you to take you into an unconscious state so you could heal."

"Montana, who did that to your face? Did Mercy come after you again? I'll talk to Eddy. He and I will end their abuse, once and for all."

As he spoke, I could see him struggling with his restraints and felt it best to let Dr. Kelso give the explanations required.

"No worries right now, big brother... I'll get the nurse and the doc, and then we can talk."

The nurse came in and checked his vitals and allowed him some water, then went off with the doctor's instructions for a modified diet for his first meal in four days. The doc spent some time with Ace alone. By the time I was allowed back in the room, two hours had passed.

Ace appeared fine and was sitting up in bed; he gave me a sheepish grin when I entered the room. I sat on the side of his bed and gave him a hug. I squeezed him tight for a long time. Long enough for him to finally break down and cry. He sobbed for I don't know how long.

Through it all, I didn't shed a single tear. Nor was I moved to do so by his tears. I was simply and mechanically there for him. What felt like hours later, he stopped. He was done and I thought he would be okay. Well, okay enough that he could function without being a danger to himself or anyone else.

I was right, and the next day Eddy arrived to pick us up and take us home.

I hadn't seen my other two brothers since we had received the news five days earlier. I had spoken to both Eddy and Adam several times, but not to Alex or Danny.

Subconsciously, I think I did it as a self-protection thing. Despite feeling wooden and seeing myself in that light, Alex would have seen the truth. So would Adam, of course, if he hadn't been so busy looking after Danny. In fact, it seemed that destiny had allowed me to stay hidden from them.

Our home looked like a floral shop; we could barely get the front door open for all the flowers and cards that the community had brought over. Apparently there were enough cooked meals delivered to last a month. That was one thing I sure loved about where I lived. It was the third most overpopulated city in North America but it had the soul of a small community. The next few days were taken up with funeral arrangements, meetings with lawyers, etc. Adam, who was staying at the house to help in any way he could, was a real help to Ace with all the details of the arrangements.

He was with us at the lawyer's and at the funeral home. He had paid close attention at dinner that night and I'd have to say he probably did eighty percent of the work.

"Thank God for Adam," Ace said, several times throughout those days following his release from the hospital. I agreed, but hardly showed it. Everything that happened was from a distance. I was watching everything, but I wasn't really there.

The funeral came and went, and the week following, Alex and I went back to school. It had only been two weeks since we had been here, but it felt like a lifetime ago. I avoided everyone I could and only participated in the simplest of conversations. Things were not the same and I didn't expect that they would be ever again.

Alex threw himself into his music with a renewed fervour. He had mourned but he was still upset and feeling the loss of Dad, probably reliving the loss of Mom. I knew he couldn't feel me right now and it bothered him. But being the guy he was he kept his feelings to himself and expressed it in music instead.

My grades slid real fast. I had not mourned, as I have already said. I was still locked within myself. I couldn't write music. I quit dancing and the cheerleading squad—handed it over to Chrissie. I skipped out of classes and went for long walks through Stanley Park. I felt as if I was looking for something but was not sure what.

The only thing I didn't quit was the band but I played with no passion. I'm sure Alex and Otter noticed. But we seemed to have this unspoken agreement that the "Dad" topic was taboo. Don't get me wrong, sometimes it was work to stay wooden, dead. I started smoking pot and drank more rum than ever, and basically didn't give a crap about anything.

I wouldn't talk to Adam unless he was standing right in front of me. Ace would rant and threaten me with everything you can imagine; I would only stare during these episodes until he had yelled himself out. Then I would simply walk away.

Finally, Adam called in the big guns, Dr. Treakle, and said I was expected down at the hospital for an appointment. I no-showed and then I was told that if I didn't choose to go willingly, I would be forced. I went into hiding, not telling anyone where I was.

I went to my West Side buddies, the ones who didn't know my boyfriend or my big scary brother. Shelley hid me at her place and played dumb as to my whereabouts when Alex came looking for me. I attended a West Side Halloween party with Shelley two days after Alex had come looking for me.

I had Shelley scout out the party for any West Enders, but none were there. Most of our ties had severed with Ralph's death. I was going to use this as my opportunity to end my life. By the time anyone found me, it would be too late.

Dressed as the Grim Reaper I put on my happy face, so as not to alert anyone to my true mental state. At some point, I wandered away from the party and headed to the UBC woods. I found a soft spot under a maple tree and passed out.

I had strange dreams. I heard my mother talking to me. I saw Ralph and my dad, and others. Some I recognized and some I didn't recognize.

I made my way back down to Shelley's in the morning, and asked to borrow some clothes. She told me that Danny had been looking for me. He was worried as I had been gone for three nights. Shelley, who normally didn't give a shit about anything, looked at me reproachfully like I was the bad guy for making people worry.

I told her that if he or any of my brothers came by again, to tell them I was going where they couldn't follow.

I gave myself away by being so cryptic but I was confident that I could get to Jericho Beach before any of them found me, and I did. I headed straight for the water. I was in the freezing water up to my shoulders when someone called my name. I dove down and struggled to the bottom, clinging to the rock I had carried out with me to keep myself submerged. I felt myself let go. I saw a tunnel in the water. Through the tunnel, I saw what must have been paradise.

Just as I reached out my hand to enter the tunnel, I was suddenly yanked. "No!" My mind screamed, leave me be. It was no use, however. I was lifeless, and couldn't fight away my rescuer. My rescuer's hand became two and I was being dragged to the surface of the water.

I saw all this from my vantage point above my body. The soul that was me, hovering in interest. Then abruptly everything stopped.

Chapter 27

November 1981

The pictures of the past stopped abruptly. I was back to where I had begun. I remembered in my dream state Dad asking me to choose life. Choose, why? I thought. This is my chance, to let go, be free of pain, never to feel the loss of myself, or anyone else again. But what and who would I be leaving behind? Was that worth the pain I'd been running from?

Eddy and other friends appeared, and I smiled as I watched them parade in front of me. Ace, Danny and Alex were next. I saw them as they were and then I saw them as how they might be if I were to die. That last picture was almost too much to bear.

Adam was next and my heart filled at the sight of him. He was so beautiful... and then I saw more, a possible future. Adam and I got married and he wore a kilt. In another flash we were at a beautiful beach house. I saw Ace and Alex happily married and Danny engaged, and me pregnant. Oh my goodness.

Alex on a plane and us playing music on a stage before a huge crowd of thousands of people. We were playing to a crowd of thousands.

My brothers at my funeral looked so old and haggard I barely recognized them, didn't recognize them. Alex looked at me, directly in the eyes and his eyes were dead. Adam's light had gone out and he no longer painted. I saw him working for his father in construction. Years later in his forties, he looked sad and miserable. I saw myself next, all of my life from the beginning to now. I saw all my actions, all my selfish indulgences and all of the times my ego controlled my actions and reactions. What I had done to my family because I couldn't get past myself. I was always in my way because I just couldn't accept anything.

Dad made a sudden appearance.

"That's only a sampling, Peanut, of the many incredible things that lie in store for you. Wake up now, darling, wake up and choose life."

November 18, 1981

I opened my eyes to a very bright room. I felt like a time traveler. Waking up in this strange place seemed so surreal. I had no idea how long I had been here, or how long my travels back through this past year and a half had taken. I felt older, like I had lived a century in however long I had been unconscious.

The journey had brought me to a greater understanding. I was ready to live. I was not just a baby born to my two creators who made me. I was choosing to live and that was a game changer for me. I turned my head and observed vases of flowers and cards. Every surface covered., evidence that some time had passed. I felt so active on the inside for the first time since prior to Dad's death. My body felt horrible, but a happiness filled me that even my sore body couldn't take from me and despite the aches and pains, I was happy to be alive. Happy to feel and grateful to know I was here and the universe, or God, or my parents in heaven, had a plan for me.

I slowly turned my head to the chair beside my bed and there was Ace, slumped over in a chair too small for his physique. My lips were cracked and I wasn't even going to attempt to speak until I had some water. I looked for something to make noise to get his attention.

My side table was just within reach of my fingertips. There was a Styrofoam cup there with a bit of water and I was able to tip it. As it landed on the floor what little contents were in the cup spilled. As I hoped, it woke up Ace.

He opened his eyes and looked directly at me. He stared as if not seeing I was awake. He rubbed his eyes and looked again... and was just about to fall back asleep when I managed a little squeak from my parched throat.

A broad grin spread across his face. "The Sun will come out tomorrow"- The lyrics from that Broadway show Annie came to mind at the happiness I saw in my brother's face.

He was out of his chair and over hugging me in seconds. "Peanut, I knew you would come back."

I grinned, my lips cracking more, but that was okay. I was alive and happy to be so. Moments later, Ace went to let the doc know I was awake.

"How long?" I croaked, when he came back. "How long," I swallowed as I tried again, "have I been here?"

"About three weeks, Peanut. Danny found you and brought you in on November first. It's November eighteenth today. Thank the gods you came back. How are you?" He asked me hesitantly.

"Fantastic," I croaked and gave him one of my famous side grins.

"Really, you're okay? Hmm, how old are you?"

I laughed, and then coughed a bit. "Last time I checked I was sixteen, but seventeen will be along soon, poor you," I teased.

He grinned. "I'm ready for it. Bring it on, Montana the terror. I've got to phone Dan and Alex. They've been so sad and this news will really cheer them up."

Before I could respond he was out the door and I pondered what Dad had shown me. Already many of the things he had shown me were vague, like a dream. There were snippets of scenes but I couldn't remember it all right now, but perhaps one day I would.

Life was worth it, I thought, and not because of what I had seen but because of who was in my life. I got to be me and it didn't matter who didn't accept me for who I was because, for the moment at least, I did and for the moment, that was all that mattered.

This was my life and I was going to make it exactly how I wanted, and for now that's all I needed to know. It seemed like only moments passed and all three of my brothers were in the room bouncing and jostling me in their attempts to feel me and make sure I was really there.

Adam was right behind the guys when they came into the hospital room. He hugged me and smiled, but I could tell he was holding back. Who could blame him? I had pushed him so far away from me; I didn't expect Adam to forgive me or take me back, muse or no.

After the hospital—after Adam knew I was going to make it—I didn't see him. He didn't call, and I didn't call. He didn't drop by and I couldn't possibly stop by to see him. I was beginning to think my old man had lied to me to get me to live. That everything he had shared was a lie.

I wanted to call him so many times and apologize and as usual, I couldn't get past my own shame to do it. I let that feeling get in the way. I wanted to tell him that I loved him. That I would love him forever. It didn't seem right, though, after what I had put him through.

Three weeks passed and it was getting close to Christmas. One night I was downtown shopping for gifts and saw that the Vogue Theatre was playing *Grease (the original)* in honour of *Grease Two* being released in '82. I wanted to reminisce, feel closer to that girl I had left behind. I enjoyed it just as much as the first time. When it was over, I started for home. It was later and I was enjoying the quiet darkness, the anonymity, and like the first time, I was busy musing and not paying much attention to my surroundings.

I was thinking of John Travolta in his black outfit at the end, so sexy, when I saw a black 280Z following me. How ironic, I thought, just like the car Adam was driving when he followed me from the movie theatre that first time we had met. The car turned a corner and was forgotten. My thoughts consumed with Adam.

A block later the same car pulled over beside and and the window came down.

"Hey, aren't you Danny's little sister?" a familiar voice asked.

"Yeah, what's it to ya?" I asked in my toughest voice.

"Hey, ease up, I was at the same movie as you. *Grease*, right? I thought you might want a ride home. It's getting dark, and I'm sure your brothers are worried about you."

He didn't need to say another word. I got in the car and turned to face him.

"Adam."

"Montana, you don't have to explain anything to me," he said, as he headed onto the bridge for the west side. "This is a do-over, or a new beginning, however you want to look at it."

And like magic, we were us once again. No strangeness, no walls between us. Just back as if no time had passed at all.

"Where are we going?"

"I thought I would take you to my place," he said with a grin. "We have a lot of catching up to do."

I felt a familiar heat in my belly at his words and visualized what being alone with him may mean. Maybe this time, all the pent up tension I felt when we were close would be released.

"Hurry."

Adam looked at me questioningly.

"I want you," I answered simply.

We arrived at Adam's. He opened a bottle of wine and passed me a glass, lit some candles, turned on some music and then sat facing me on his couch.

"Did you follow me, Adam, or did you just happen to see me exiting the theatre?"

"Montana, you know me better than that. I knew you were Christmas shopping and I knew you would go to that movie. And like the first time, I sat a few rows away from you, watching your face as you watched the movie."

"Why do you watch me?"

"Because when I watch you I capture the essence of the world through your beautiful face. You're my muse, in art, in life, in all things. One day, Montana, you and I will say our vows and create an amazing life together."

Those words sparked a memory from when I was unconscious. I remembered what my Dad said and an image of an older Adam wearing a kilt. I moved from my seat beside him and straddled him.

He gripped my hair gently and tugged my head closer, his lips soft as they descended on mine. A shudder moved through me and a slow burn was felt throughout my entire being. He took his time and everything new felt different but also really good.

Adam touched all my forbidden places and my heart soared with the new sensations. When my body finally crashed like the waves upon the sand, I was different. Our visceral connection ended, but he kept me in the present. His eyes watched as I completely relaxed and melted into the warm mattress.

He hadn't missed a single expression and I knew he was memorizing all of it so he could paint it later. My first time forever immortalized on canvas.

"Oh, my, god, Adam, I feel so different." He lowered himself to the mattress and tugged me to his side. We cuddled in the aftermath of our first time together. The feelings and sensations made all those silly love songs finally make sense.

"Montana, are you okay?"

"I am amazing, so amazing. I don't know how to describe it. I didn't know it would be like this. It was amazing."

He grinned. "Was it worth the wait?"

"Yes, oh, yes, yes," I answered. "Is it always like this?"

He laughed. "Only time will tell. Here, have some water, Montana." Apparently, hydration was still on the to do list. I did, and asked him if I was going home and if I wasn't, did I need to call? Again, he smiled and told me it had all been taken care of. I was his for the entire weekend.

"Montana, I have a confession. I have loved you since the first time I heard your name leave your brother's lips."

"I know Adam, you already told me. Speaking of lips, I want nothing else but yours on mine."

"Good," he answered as he pulled me on top of him. "Kiss me and keep kissing me."

"That's my plan," but even as I said it, I knew our story wouldn't be so cut and dried. It was only just beginning.

The End

Acknowledgements

Thank you to my West End tribe for a speedy childhood and one I wouldn't trade for the world.

Thank you to my friend and publisher, Deborah of Rottie Books for being invested in my vision.

Thank you to L.G. Knight of Alluring Blurbs for her work on the blurbs for this anthology. I love them!

Thank you to my Alpha Team, Angie Goodin, Lori Smith, L.G. Knight, Rose Chaplan, Denise Holder and Anice Walker, and my ARC & Street Team for taking the time to review and share my work.

Thank you to my readers for your ongoing support.

And last but not least, a shout out to Western Sky for all her hard work and creative genius.

In love & light, Rogue London xo

About Rogue London

Rogue London is an International best selling author of sassy, steamy, suspenseful romance that features alpha men with a soft spot for the women they inevitably fall for.

Rogue's imagination is limitless for exploring the power exchange dynamic in her stories.

https://linktr.ee/RogueLondonmedia

About N.M. McGregor

N.M. McGregor is a Canadian author born in the east and bred in the west. Despite the huge shifts to her beloved Vancouver over the past few decades, she still loves the place that helped build who she is today.

The Inner Circle Series is a dedication with her connection to a time and place that will always hold a special place in her heart.

About the Publisher

Rottie Books was created to help developing and experienced authors take their books from draft to finished product. Our team of authors have the expertise to help you finish and launch your new creation from blurb writing to covers.

We at Rottie Books appreciate your taking the time to leave a review on the site where you purchased the book, and on Goodreads or Bookbub. Your feedback is important to our authors.
Contact us at deborah@rottiebooks.com
https://rottiebooks.com/

Manufactured by Amazon.ca
Bolton, ON

44217443R00164